KT-151-085

Fortune's
Children
THE GROOMS

*Meet the Arizona Fortunes—a family with a
legacy of wealth, influence and power. As they
gather for a host of weddings, a shocking plot
against the family is revealed…and passionate
new romances are ignited.*

DR SHANE FORTUNE: This proudly
independent loner thinks he's finally got his life
together, until a weird twist of fate brings his
former girlfriend to his house in the middle of the
night—and back into his lfe.

CYNTHIA McCREE: The single mum has put
her past firmly behind her, and nothing—not
even an undeniable passion—is going to bring
her back to the man who'd once been the love of
her life. Not when she has so much at stake…

BOBBY McCREE: This five-year-old is the most
important thing in Cynthia's life—that is, until a
midnight collision brings her smack into the arms
of his Native American father!

FORTUNE'S CHILDREN

Silhouette is proud to present more gripping love stories about this fabulously wealthy family whose legacy is greater than mere riches. Follow the Fortunes as new family members are welcomed into the fold, and long-hidden secrets and scandals are revealed…

Fortune's Children: The Grooms

Fortune's Children: The Lost Heirs

Look out for a special 3-in-1 volume at Christmas:

FORTUNE'S
SECRET CHILD

Shawna Delacorte

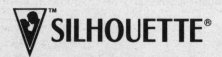

*First published in Great Britain 2002
Silhouette Books, Eton House, 18-24 Paradise Road,
Richmond, Surrey TW9 1SR*

© Harlequin Books S.A. 2000

*Special thanks and acknowledgement are given to Shawna Delacorte
for her contribution to Fortune's Children: The Grooms mini-series.*

ISBN 0 373 76324 7

26-0402

*Printed and bound in Spain
by Litografia Rosés S.A., Barcelona*

SHAWNA DELACORTE

has delayed her move to Washington State, staying in the Midwest in order to spend some additional time with family. She still travels as often as time permits, and is looking forward to visiting several new places during the forthcoming year while continuing to devote herself to writing full-time. Shawna would appreciate hearing from her readers. She can be reached at 6505 E. Central, Box No 300, Wichita, KS 67206-1924, USA.

To Judy Laivo, who has displayed such
grace in the face of adversity.

One

Cynthia McCree awoke with a start. She sat bolt upright in bed, shaking the fogginess from her head as she collected her bearings in the unfamiliar surroundings. She furrowed her brow, straining to hear the noise that had woken her. There it was again, the same sound. Her muscles tensed and an uncomfortable dryness closed off her throat. She tried to swallow her apprehension, but it refused to go away.

She slid out of bed and pulled on her robe. Her heartbeat quickened. Her stomach jittered nervously. She quietly made her way down the darkened hallway to her son's bedroom. She tried to calm her nerves by telling herself that the sound was just Bobby, having a restless night due to his new surroundings. She opened the door and stepped inside.

The night-light in the adjoining bathroom provided just enough illumination for her to see. She pulled up the sheet and tucked it around the shoulders of the sleeping five-year-old boy. She placed a tender kiss on his forehead. A soft warmth settled over her and wrapped around her senses as she watched him. He was the most important thing in her life. He'd been through so much upheaval during the past two weeks. She hoped things would settle down for him now. For both of them.

She was jerked out of her moment of reverie. There it was again. Her body stiffened, and the loving glow that had filtered through her consciousness just moments earlier was shoved aside. Her anxiety level shot up. Her heart lodged in her throat. The noise came from downstairs. Did she dare go to investigate? She glanced back at her sleeping son, then set her jaw in a hard line of determination. She drew a steadying breath, then stepped into the hallway.

Downstairs in the kitchen Shane Fortune had just popped a frozen dinner into the microwave. He leaned back against the counter and closed his eyes. The weariness from the long day had finally caught up with him. The three-day medical conference was exhausting enough without tackling the one-hundred-mile drive from Phoenix back to his home in Pueblo, Arizona.

A sound broke the quiet, yanking him out of his thoughts. An adrenaline surge put his senses on full alert. Someone had stepped on the squeaky stair between the foyer and the second floor. He made his way from the kitchen, through the utility room and down the back hall, arriving at the arched opening underneath the stairs. He paused for a moment as his eyes adjusted to the dim illumination filtering in through the windows from the outside street light.

A shadowy figure crossed the foyer toward the front door. Shane moved silently through the darkness in much the same way as a cat stalks its prey, or as one of his Native American ancestors would have stealthily picked his way through a rocky canyon. He sprang from behind, knocking the intruder to the ground. He easily pinned the struggling body against the terra-cotta floor in the entry-way. Then his hand grazed a decidedly female breast and he heard a woman gasp.

Shane yanked his hand away. He focused on the face of the intruder. Her identity exploded in his consciousness, leaving him frozen in stunned silence. Waves of conflict-ing emotions swept through him. He had not seen her in six years, but there was no mistaking who she was even in the darkened surroundings. No one had eyes like hers, eyes that seemed to glow an iridescent blue. He couldn't find enough breath even to speak. He finally forced out one word, managing only a hushed whisper. "Cynthia."

He hovered directly above her, their mouths almost in contact. Sexual electricity leapt between them. It was the same sensual excitement that had once been part of their life together. It wrenched all the old emotions from the past—both good ones and bad—and deposited them in the here and now. What weird twist of fate had brought her to his house in the middle of the night?

She stopped struggling, but her muscles remained tensed. Every heated desire he had ever felt for Cynthia McCree came rushing back full force. Memories of long ago—the smell of her perfume, the taste of her mouth, the feel of her naked body pressed along the length of his, the many passion-filled nights of lovemaking—came from the same hidden place that also held old feelings of confusion and anger.

Cynthia wasn't sure if any of this was real or only a cruel trick of her mind prompted by her return to Pueblo. Shane Fortune…was it possible that she was still in bed fast asleep and this was only a bad dream? She felt his heartbeat as his body pressed against hers—at least, she thought it was his heartbeat. It could just as easily have been her own. Their lips were so close she could almost feel the contact. All the old emotions flooded over her—times of unbridled passion and times of deep sorrow. He had been the love of her life. He was also the man who had broken her heart and hurt her more than she thought possible.

None of this made sense. She shook off the past and renewed her struggle as she tried to collect her wits. She shoved hard against his chest with both hands in an effort to push him away. She had to pull herself together and do it quickly. There was a lot more at stake here than being physically thrown together with the last man on earth she had expected to be with or even wanted to be with.

She noticed a moment of hesitation on his part when he resisted her efforts to dislodge him. It almost seemed as if he intended to close the few inches of space separating their mouths. A sharp jolt of fear surged through her body—not fear of what Shane might do, but rather fear that she would be a willing accomplice. Then as suddenly as it had all begun, he relinquished his hold on her and stood up. A very shaken Cynthia scrambled to her feet, then leaned against the staircase banister to steady her wobbly legs. She gasped for breath as anxiety ran rampant through her body. She kept a wary eye on him while he reached for a light switch.

Shane's logical and analytical mind tried to dismiss the emotions and put things into some type of order. He couldn't make any sense of what had happened. He had not been this confused since the day he'd told Cynthia they had no future together and their affair was over. Those years had been very intense for him, filled with inner turmoil and conflicts. He had cut her out of his life with surgical efficiency, and there had been no further contact between them—until now. He didn't like the nervous uncertainty that jittered inside him. He clicked on a light, then took a calming breath before turning to face her.

He tried to speak, but his throat constricted, trapping his words inside. The disarray of her long blond hair exuded an earthy sexuality that caught him totally off guard. The barefoot woman in a knee-length robe standing in front of him was even more beautiful than the memory he'd been carrying around for six years. A wave of desire surged through his body, in direct contrast to his practiced outer show of calm and control.

He tried to beat down this unaccustomed lack of composure and take charge of the situation the same way he did with everything that came his way. It was a skill he'd perfected over a lifetime, making sure no one could read his thoughts or feelings. Before he could manage it, though, Cynthia usurped any thought he had of being in control of the circumstances.

She made no effort to curb the edge of displeasure surrounding her words. "Just what do you think you're doing here?"

A sudden twinge of discomfort reinforced her awareness of the way she was dressed. Cynthia tightened the sash of her robe and pulled the collar close around her neck. She was vaguely aware of the scrape on her forearm, the result of contact with the rough tile floor. She put as much authority into her voice as she could dredge up from her rapidly dwindling reserve of confidence. "I made sure the doors were locked before going to bed. How did you get in here?"

As a corporate attorney, she had learned to read people. She immediately recognized his body language—leaning forward in an attempt to psychologically throw her off balance, the unsettling way his dark piercing eyes seemed to see inside her, his attempt to control the situation and control her. It had worked back when her worldly experience was limited to Pueblo, Arizona, but it wasn't going to work anymore. She had long since become toughened by the realities of life. She pulled her determination together, held her ground and refused to back down before his aggressive manner.

"You're asking how *I* got in?" Had he heard her correctly? Was she really challenging his right to be in his own house? None of this made any sense to him. He maintained his outer facade of total authority as he scrambled to put things into some kind of perspective. "I think a better question is, What are *you* doing in *my* house?"

Her eyes widened in shock. She stumbled backward a couple of steps. Her breath caught in her throat as she tried to speak, giving her voice a husky sound. "Your house? This is *your* house?" The tightness in her jaw relaxed a little. Disbelief covered her features where determination had been just a moment earlier. "How can that possibly be?"

The sharpness in her words melted away as it turned into bewilderment. She seemed to be staring into space rather than focusing on anything. She sounded almost as if she was trying to work out a problem in her mind rather than talking to him. "Kate insisted that I stay here until I get everything settled and find a job. With my mother having died when I was a child, I'm the one responsible for handling my father's estate. Kate led me to believe that she owned this house, that it was leased to someone who was going to be out of state for a while."

She struggled to regain her determination, finally managing to exercise some authority over what was happening, even though the situation was far from clear. She stared at him, her manner no longer questioning or unsure. "She certainly didn't tell me this house belonged to you."

His brow knitted in a frown. He shook his head, hoping the puzzle pieces would settle into their proper places. "Kate Fortune said you could stay in my house? Your father's estate? What's going on here?" Shane took a calming breath. On more than one occasion over the past six years he had envisioned a reunion with Cynthia and pondered what might have been had he not cut her out of his life. The thoughts always wound up making him feel sad, so he had refused to dwell on them. Only now here she suddenly was, the flesh-and-blood woman, more beautiful than ever—not a figment of his imagination—and he didn't know how to handle it.

He motioned for her to follow him into the kitchen. "I must be missing something. It's been a couple of weeks since I talked to Kate. I told her I would be attending a medical conference up in Phoenix. I wasn't scheduled to be home until tomorrow but decided to drive back tonight, instead."

Cynthia glanced nervously toward the top of the stairs. She didn't want their voices to wake Bobby. Things were awkward enough without her son making an unexpected appearance. She returned her attention to Shane, thankful they were moving away from the bottom of the stairs. Things were becoming more and more bizarre by the minute. Her initial trepidation had turned to confusion and now bordered on anger.

And then, as if to mock her attempt at control, her suppressed desire for Shane Fortune heated to an uncomfortable level. She tried to keep any and all emotion out of her voice. She was an intelligent adult who could certainly handle an awkward situation with a former lover in a mature manner. At least that was what she tried to convince herself of. "I don't know how this apparent misunderstanding occurred, but there's obviously a problem here, and it needs to be straightened out immediately."

"I'll have to agree with you on that." Shane took his dinner from the microwave and set it on the counter, then turned his attention back to Cynthia. He felt a twinge of guilt when he noticed the scrape on her arm. It was not the first time he had battled feelings of guilt where Cynthia McCree was concerned.

He watched her for a moment as she nervously smoothed her hair back with her hands—the curve of her jaw, the tilt of her nose, the soft lips, the creamy skin. His breathing quickened and then his throat went dry, making it difficult for him to swallow. He finally looked away, hoping to break the bands of tension that tightened across his chest. He didn't know what to think and wasn't sure what he felt.

He glanced at the dinner he had removed from the microwave, then shoved it aside. Food was of no interest to him at that moment. He stared at her, drinking in her beauty as he tried to sort out what had happened.

He desperately wanted to reach out and touch her—to caress her cheek and to hold her in his arms—but he didn't dare. It took all his willpower to fight the urge. He glanced away from the emotional pull of her presence. He wasn't sure how to proceed but felt pressured to say something. "So...start at the beginning and tell me how you came to be in my house."

She nervously shifted her weight from one foot to the other. Her confidence faded with each passing second. She could not keep the uncertainty out of her voice. "You own this house? Is this also where you live...your permanent residence?"

"I live here three hundred and sixty-five days a year,

three hundred and sixty-six in leap years.'' He leveled a steady gaze at her. ''And just how long have you been living here?''

She stared at the floor as she uttered a sheepish response. ''I moved in late this afternoon.''

''Exactly what is this all about?''

His attitude was demanding, but in light of the circumstances, Cynthia had to admit his request was not unreasonable. She took a calming breath and attempted to put the facts into some sort of logical order, an easier task than tackling her need to set aside the very disconcerting effect Shane Fortune had on her—even after all these years. A tremor made its way through her body, telling her just how desirable she still found him.

''My father died three days ago,'' she began.

''I'm sorry.'' His surprise was genuine and his words sincere. ''I didn't know. Had he been ill?''

''Apparently so—'' a sob caught in her throat ''—but he hadn't said anything about not feeling well...'' Her voice trailed off, her despair over the loss of her father momentarily distracting her. ''Anyway—'' she returned her attention to Shane, determined to present a strong front ''—late one night I received a phone call from his neighbor saying he had found my father unconscious in the hall and called an ambulance to take him to the hospital. I finally got hold of the doctor.''

She steeled herself. Her personal concerns and feelings about her father's death were private and certainly not any of Shane's business. She tried to tamp down her anxiety and steady her nerves before continuing.

''I was making some changes in my life's direction and personal priorities and was already packed up to move,'' she said, ''so it was a simple matter to put my household goods in storage to be shipped later. I packed the bare essentials in my car and drove straight from Chicago to Pueblo.''

''Chicago… So that's your car with the Illinois license plates parked on the street in front of the house?''

''Yes.'' She snapped out the answer, annoyed at the way the conversation had strayed from the problem at hand. ''Anyway, I had assumed I could stay at my father's, but when I arrived, I found that his *house* was really a small studio apartment in a building that looked like it should have been condemned.'' She still had difficulty accepting what had been going on with her father. She clenched her jaw and fought back her tears before they could escape.

She forced out her words, preferring to dictate the direction of the conversation rather than giving him the opportunity to ask questions. ''I tried to get some information from his neighbor, but he didn't say anything that explained what had happened.'' She slowly shook her head, trying to put logic to something that refused to make sense. ''There was no way I could stay there, so I rented a studio apartment on a weekly basis at a motel close to the hospital. My father died four days later without ever regaining consciousness.'' A sob caught in her throat as the pain of her loss forced itself to the surface. ''He didn't even know I was there.'' She paused, then tucked her private moment of sorrow safely away where no one could see it.

She looked up at Shane, squared her shoulders and gathered her composure again. ''Then Kate offered me this house to stay in until I could get my father's estate straightened out, find a place to live and get a job.''

''It's amazing that we didn't run into each other at the hospital. I'm on staff there.''

''Yes, I know.'' Her voice dropped to a soft whisper. ''I saw your name on the registry.''

An awkward silence filled the air before Shane finally

broke it. "Well, that certainly explains what you're doing in Pueblo, but it doesn't explain how you and Kate got together. I can't imagine her doing something like *giving* my house to someone." As soon as the words left his mouth, he knew he had made a colossal blunder. They sounded way too harsh, especially in light of the circumstances of her father's death. He saw her eyes narrow and her jaw tighten, but it was too late to take the words back.

She sharply clipped her words, unable to keep the anger out of her voice. "Kate didn't *give* me a house. I can afford to pay my own way. I don't require charity from anyone, least of all from the Fortune family. I told Kate I would pay rent while I was here."

"No one said you were asking for charity." The volume of his voice rose to match hers. "That still doesn't tell me how and why you and Kate even got together."

She spit out the words without making any attempt to hold back her anger. "I don't need your permission before speaking with someone." She glared at him. "But for your information she read the obituary notice in the newspaper. It mentioned the graveside service that took place this morning." Her voice softened as thoughts and feelings from several years ago again invaded her consciousness. "I was surprised to see her there. I had only met her briefly on a couple of occasions back when you and I..."

The memory of their two-year intense love affair, which she'd thought would last a lifetime, brought her words to a halt. She swallowed her momentary lapse and continued, though a lot of the fire had gone out of her attitude. The captivating and tantalizing presence of the very tempting Shane Fortune was playing havoc with her reality. Her emotions had been on a roller-coaster ride from the moment she realized the identity of the man who had tackled her. She needed to bring the wild ride to a halt.

"Well, anyway, I was surprised to see her at the service. It never occurred to me that she would remember who I was or associate me with the newspaper obit for my father."

He folded his arms across his chest and leveled a steady gaze at her. "I see." His words may not have said it, but his attitude and tone of voice spelled out his skepticism.

She scowled fiercely. "Since you apparently choose not to believe me, I suggest you take the matter up with Kate rather than continuing to badger me. I certainly don't have any other reason for being in your house."

His voice grew louder still. "I did *not* say I didn't believe you. Stop putting words in my mouth." His voice dropped. "And I'm not badgering you."

She put her hands on her hips, and her voice rose, her anger spilling out in each word. "I'm hardly putting words in your mouth." She stole a quick glance out the kitchen door toward the staircase. She lowered her tone, but her ire had not been assuaged. "And I'd appreciate it if you'd keep your voice down so you don't wake Bobby." A sinking feeling settled inside her. The words had slipped out before she could censor them.

"Bobby? You mean there's someone *else* in my house besides you?" Shane's reaction was immediate—curiosity combined with a determination that said he was about to tackle a problem head on. "Just who is this Bobby? Your boyfriend?" He hesitated, his words more cautious than accusatory, as if he was uncertain about saying them. "Your husband?"

She tried to still her apprehension. She could not keep the quaver out of her voice, nor could she look Shane in the eye. She stared at the floor and uttered a barely audible response. "Bobby is my son."

"Your...your *son?*" Shane staggered backward a couple of steps, stunned. He came to a halt when he bumped into the pantry door. "I didn't realize you had married."

"I'm not married." She attempted to change the subject, making no effort to keep the irritation out of voice. The sick churning in the pit of her stomach confirmed that she was a long way from being in control of anything. "Now, if the inquisition is over…"

He regarded her for a second as he switched his attitude from personal to detached. "You've certainly changed." He had to do something to get his rampaging emotions under control. He knew his anger was only one of them, a small one at that. The overriding element—the thing that bothered him the most and what he had to curb—was his all-consuming desire for Cynthia McCree. It was something he thought he would never come face-to-face with again, yet here it was. "We never used to argue about anything."

"If you mean that I'm no longer that docile young woman you knew when we were pursuing the education for our careers, the one who hung on your every word, then you're right—I've changed. I learned about the *real* world very quickly." She shot him a pointed look. "Almost overnight." She could tell she hit the mark with her reference to the abrupt way he had terminated their affair.

She straightened her stance and presented him with a businesslike facade that said she considered the conversation at an end. "You needn't worry, my son and I will be out of your house first thing in the morning." She whirled around and started toward the door, hoping she had turned away in time to prevent him from seeing the anguish that must surely have registered on her face. The last thing she wanted was to show any weakness or vulnerability to Shane Fortune.

"Wait a minute!" Shane reached out and grabbed her

arm, bringing her to a halt. Her words and tone may have been angry, but he also heard what was underneath. He heard the hurt and knew he had been the cause of it. That knowledge weighed uncomfortably on his conscience. He was not proud of what he had done to her six years ago and, in particular, the way he had done it. He had never been able to forgive himself for hurting her the way he had. Was it too late to make things right? He didn't know. He suppressed a sigh of despair. He didn't know much of anything at the moment.

She jerked her arm free of his grasp and turned a defiant stare on him. She spit out her words, along with her hurt and anger. "What now? Isn't *first thing in the morning* soon enough for you? Do you want us out of here tonight?"

"No. That's not it." He backed away from her anger and her surprisingly aggressive behavior. "It's your arm..." His manner softened. "Let me take a look at that abrasion."

Cynthia glanced at the scrape just below her elbow. What little composure she still possessed was slipping away faster than she could keep control of it. She had to get away from him. From his far-too-tempting presence. She snapped out her words. "It's nothing."

Shane grasped her arm again, this time gently, as he changed from the strong and determined Shane Fortune to the compassionate and caring Dr. Fortune. His soothing voice elicited the type of patient confidence that made him so successful and popular at the hospital. "At least let me put some antiseptic on it."

He tugged until he felt her relent. He slid his fingers down her arm, took her hand in his, then led her across the kitchen. The warmth of her skin spread through his body, rousing a combination of emotions unlike any he'd ever experienced. It was all very confusing and unsettling. He tried to concentrate on the matter at hand.

He opened a cupboard and grabbed a package of cotton balls and a bottle of antiseptic. She flinched and her muscles tensed as he applied it. His soothing voice carried his concern. "Does this hurt?"

"No...it stings a little, that's all."

It was as if all the fight had suddenly gone out of her and a crisis had passed. He continued to cling to her hand. He had never forgotten the sensual feeling he got from touching her, yet the tingling sensation emanating from his fingertips and continuing up his arm carried all the excitement of something new and wonderful. The sensation both thrilled and disturbed him.

Cynthia worked her hand out of his grasp without actually jerking it away. His touch stirred up emotions and needs she thought she'd safely buried away. She tried to physically distance herself from his commanding presence and his tempting allure, which made her pulse jump and her blood race. She put as much confidence into her voice as she could muster. "As I said, my son and I will be out of your house first thing in the morning." She turned and practically ran from him.

"Cynthia, wait." He watched helplessly as she left the kitchen and started up the stairs, ignoring his words. He stood motionless, rooted to the spot, as the most exciting and tantalizing woman he had ever known walked away from him just as he had walked away from her six long years ago.

He didn't have a clue what to do. Shane Fortune—the man whose life was totally under control, the man who knew exactly where he was going and what he was doing, the man whose commanding presence inspired confidence in everyone around him—was at a complete loss. He stared at the spot where she'd been standing just a moment earlier, an escalating sense of loss tugging at his consciousness, revealing the emptiness that lived inside him. He realized he had no one to blame but himself.

He and Cynthia had met in graduate school. He thought back. She had been part of his life at a time when he had been trying to deal with inner turmoil about his dual heritage and his place in the overall scheme of things. He had struggled to find his own identity in a life that straddled two worlds—the one on his grandfather's side, with the wealth and prestige of the Fortune family, and on the other side the Native American culture of his Tohono O'odham grandmother. He'd been positive that Cynthia would never be able to fit into that divided world, especially when he didn't know where or how he fit into it himself. It had been a time of pent-up anger and inner turmoil, which he had successfully kept hidden behind a facade of strength and control.

There had never been any confusion about his career. Unlike his brother and two cousins, he had made the decision not to work in the family-owned company, Fortune Construction. Being a doctor was what he had always wanted. His personal life, however, had been a mass of confusion and contradictions. No one really knew what he was going through back then. He had managed to keep his turmoil well hidden from everyone who knew him, including his family and Cynthia McCree.

A small spot of warmth, fueled by a long-suppressed emotional need, flickered to life. He did know one thing for certain—no matter how dark something had seemed to him, all his problems would disappear when he held Cynthia McCree in his arms. It had taken several months of stubborn denial and agonizing over what he had done before he finally admitted to himself that by leaving her he had made a colossal blunder, missed her very much and wanted her back in his life.

He had eventually swallowed his pride and asked her father where she had gone. He vividly recalled Robert McCree's angry words. *Don't you think you've already hurt her enough? I told her no good would come of associating with you. If she wants to talk to you, she knows where to find you. Everyone knows where to find the illustrious Fortunes.* The words had been cloaked in bitter sarcasm and they had hit their mark. They left him with a gaping hole in his life that had never been refilled.

He shoved aside the unpleasant memories and turned his attention to his now cold dinner. He stared at it, emitted a sigh of resignation, then put it in the refrigerator. What had been hunger pangs an hour ago had turned into uncertainty about what would happen in the morning. He busied himself with the physical activity of cleaning up the kitchen and restoring everything to its proper place. The memories continued to linger in his mind, mixing with thoughts of what the immediate future held.

He left the kitchen and started up the stairs toward his bedroom. He paused at the top of the staircase. The doors were closed at two of the four guest bedrooms. One of them was Cynthia's and the other was her son. He stopped outside the closed doors and listened for a moment. A deep disappointment had jabbed at his consciousness when she said she had a son. He continued down the hallway to his bedroom suite. A strange sense of loss overcame him as the disappointment turned to sadness.

Cynthia heard the soft footsteps outside her bedroom. She held her breath and waited in the darkness. Tears welled up in her eyes and a terrible foreboding settled over her. Would he open the door? She finally heard him move away. She closed her eyes and tried to concentrate on getting some sleep, but to no avail. Her efforts only produced an image of Shane's handsome features and the memory of many nights of heated passion. He'd been the man she thought she'd be with for the rest of her life, a love she thought would live forever. Then her entire life had come crashing down around her.

She squeezed her eyes tightly shut in an attempt to drive the image from her mind. He had rejected her, and even after all these years the pain was still very real. But that was not the most compelling issue at hand. Seeing him again had done more than resurrect heated desires and inflamed emotions. It had shoved her greatest fear to the front of the line, an all-consuming dread that nearly paralyzed her with fright. A sick churning tried to work its way up her throat. Her most closely guarded secret must be protected at all costs.

She could never allow Shane Fortune to know that he was the father of her son. She had to do everything in her power to make sure Bobby was not subjected to the same emotional upheaval she had been through, followed by the inevitable painful rejection.

Shane had terminated their relationship before she knew she was pregnant. He had rejected her, cut her out of his life with a finality that left no room for questions. It was an action that had slammed the door shut on any possibility of a discussion about what had gone wrong. For a long time she questioned herself about what she'd done that had driven him away. It wasn't until after her son was born that she stopped blaming herself for a decision that was entirely Shane's.

Cynthia knew she could not avoid running into Shane after she moved back to Pueblo, but she never dreamed it would be in such a dramatic and unsettling manner. She had only given superficial thought to what she would do when she did run into him, without speculating too much about the circumstances. The situation now dictated that she needed to make some hard decisions.

Did she owe Shane the opportunity to know his son? Was it possible to reveal the truth without Bobby being an innocent pawn caught in the middle? Could she prevent her son from being hurt the way she had been?

All she had were questions—and her fears. She had no answers.

Two

Shane paused at the top of the stairs. The house was quiet, just as it was every morning, only today was different. He was not alone in the house. Apparently Cynthia and her son were still asleep. He couldn't suppress a little snort of resentment. A decent night's sleep was more than he'd been able to accomplish. He had tossed and turned after going to bed, waking every thirty minutes or so. He didn't know what the morning would bring and wasn't at all sure he was prepared to face it.

Heading for the den, Shane intended to open the sliding doors and let in the fresh morning air. He hadn't taken more than two steps across the room when he came to an abrupt halt. A little boy lay sprawled on his stomach in front of the bookcase. It was a sight that gave him quite a start, grabbing his senses as much as his attention. He'd assumed her son was two or maybe three years old. This boy appeared to be about five.

A hard jolt of an indecipherable something shot through

his body, leaving an uncomfortable sensation in its wake, a possibility he refused to consider. She must have gotten pregnant immediately *after* their breakup. She had gone from him straight to another man's bed. A spark of rancor ignited, but was quickly extinguished by an overriding reality. Perhaps, just perhaps, he had driven her into another man's arms—someone who had gotten her pregnant, then deserted her. It was an unsettling thought, and he felt something between guilt and anger.

Shane studied the boy for a moment. He was dressed in pajamas, his light brown hair still sleep-tousled. He had surrounded himself with every one of Shane's Native American artifacts that had been within reach on the shelves. He seemed to be absorbed in a book, carefully studying each picture before turning the page to the next.

A moment of sorrow swept over Shane. Cynthia's son looked so much like her. He wondered how things might have turned out if he hadn't— He clenched his jaw and bit off the rest of the errant thought. The past couldn't be changed. It served no purpose to speculate.

The little boy looked up at him, as if suddenly aware of his presence. The sight pulled at Shane's heart and left him momentarily speechless. The boy had his mother's eyes, the same iridescent blue. Shane knew he should say something, but didn't know what. Bobby solved the problem by speaking first.

"Who are you?"

"I'm Shane Fortune. This is my house. I live here."

"My name's Bobby McCree." He showed an open curiosity, with no signs of apprehension about Shane's presence.

Bobby *McCree*. Well, that took care of whether Cynthia had ever been married to the boy's father. Realizing that left him every bit as unsettled as having her in his house and knowing she had a son.

The little boy continued to look up at him as if waiting for him to say something. Shane ran a hand across the back of his neck in an attempt to still the uncomfortable shiver, but it didn't help. He had developed a real bond with children and had no problem relating to them. He had spearheaded an entire hospital construction project solely for the benefit of Native American children, but at that moment he felt at a total loss for words. Too many conflicting thoughts and feelings raced through him. There'd been too many surprises all at once.

"So…Bobby, what's your book about?" He crossed the room as the boy rolled over, then scrambled to his feet. Bobby held up the book so Shane could see it. He was surprised to find that it didn't belong to Bobby, but came from his bookshelf, a volume of photographs depicting reservation life. Some of the photographs were over a hundred years old and others were modern. It was not the type of book he thought would have grabbed the attention of someone Bobby's age.

Shane took a closer look at the various items strewn around the den. In addition to drums, masks, baskets and other Native American artifacts, Bobby had scattered some of his toys on the couch and floor. There was a bright red fire truck, a police car, Old West action figures, building blocks and a couple of children's books. He again thought it odd that Bobby would ignore his own books and toys in favor of Shane's book of photographic studies.

"Do you like the pictures?"

"Yeah, they're neat." Bobby's captivating grin showed a missing front tooth.

"Are you hungry? Do you want some breakfast?" As awkward as the situation was, Shane could not deny the affinity he felt toward Cynthia's son. His curiosity about Bobby's father was again piqued. What kind of man would desert his own child—*if* that's what really happened.

A frown wrinkled Bobby's forehead. "My mommy always makes me breakfast. Do you know how to make breakfast?"

"I think I can handle it."

Bobby closed the book and carefully put it back in the bookcase in the same spot he had found it. He ran across the den and straight to the kitchen. Shane followed the boy, but stopped in his tracks at the kitchen door. What had been neat and tidy when he went to bed was now a disaster area.

Bobby had obviously been in the kitchen before Shane had come downstairs. He had pulled a chair next to the counter to climb up and open the cupboard. A carton sat on the table next to a dirty glass, and a puddle of spilled milk had dripped on the floor. He had also tried, it appeared, to take a pitcher of orange juice from the refrigerator, but had sloshed half of it on the floor between the refrigerator and the kitchen table. Apparently he'd ended up settling for a couple of cookies, as evidenced by the lid from the cookie jar shoved across the counter toward the sink and the trail of crumbs on the floor.

"It looks like you tried to make your *own* breakfast." Shane gazed at the boy, not sure whether to be irritated or amused. "Don't you think we should clean up this mess before we start something new?"

Bobby stared sheepishly at the floor before looking up at Shane. He answered in a quiet voice, "I guess so."

Shane set about cleaning the kitchen with Bobby doing his best to help. As much as he tried to stay neutral in his thoughts, every time he looked at the boy he saw Cynthia. A soft warmth enveloped his heart and spread through his chest. He again wondered about Bobby's father and what had happened between him and Cynthia. Those same thoughts tried to wander to what might have been, but he refused to play that game.

As soon as the kitchen was presentable, Shane set about fixing breakfast. He put the various items on a tray and carried it out to the patio, setting it on the table. Bobby followed him, pausing long enough to pick up the fire truck from the den floor. He set the truck on the table, then climbed onto the chair. Shane sipped his coffee and studied Bobby as the boy took a big drink from his glass of milk, then gulped his orange juice.

A scowl covered Bobby's face as he stared at his bowl of cereal. He looked up at Shane. "My mommy buys different cereal. I've never had this kind before. I don't like it."

"Why don't you taste it? You might be surprised. You might find a new kind of cereal you like." Shane offered him an encouraging smile. "If you eat all your cereal, I think I can find a doughnut for you."

"I don't bribe him to eat his breakfast."

Shane jerked around in his chair at the stern words. He had been so fixed on Bobby he had not heard Cynthia come up behind him.

She wore white tailored slacks and a short-sleeved top in a tangerine color. The silky-looking fabric caressed the same breast his hand had grazed last night. A tingling danced across his fingertips in response to the recollection. Her long blond hair was pulled back and fastened with a gold clasp at her nape. Last night she exuded the earthy sexuality he remembered so well. This morning she presented a pristine loveliness, which also lived in his memories. Either way, it caused his blood to rush a little hotter and his heart to beat faster.

He attempted to hide his thoughts and the very real emotional impact she had on him by adopting a more distant attitude. He may have been all cool control on the outside, but inside he fought off the clearly remembered sensations of the most intense love affair of his life. "I was beginning to wonder if you planned to sleep the morning away."

Cynthia ignored his pointed comment, but found it a lot more difficult to ignore his handsome features, his broad shoulders and strong arms, barely contained in the light-weight T-shirt, and his long legs, encased in faded jeans. His hair was shorter than he used to wear it, but the thick raven locks still feathered softly over his ears and across the back of his neck at collar length.

She took a steadying breath, but it did nothing to calm the conflicting emotions that raced through her body—heated desires and a quick rush of excitement when she saw Shane, followed closely by a sharp stab of alarm when she spotted Bobby with him. She tried to force a casual sound to her words while fighting off the panic that threatened to rob her of her last shreds of composure. "I see the two of you have met."

"Oh, yes. Bobby and I have met. We've already had a busy morning." Shane winked at the boy. "We've been cleaning up the mess *someone* left in the kitchen."

She nervously cleared her throat as she made her way to the other side of the table, where her son was seated. She placed her hands protectively on his shoulders. "I hope Bobby hasn't been any trouble. He doesn't usually wake up this early. It was probably the strange surroundings."

"Me and Shane fixed breakfast." Bobby stared down at his bowl. "But I don't think I like this kind of cereal."

She kissed her son on the forehead, then smoothed back his unruly hair. "I remember when you thought you didn't like waffles, either, because you thought they looked yucky. Now they're your favorite breakfast.'' She offered him an encouraging smile. "Don't you think you should taste the cereal before you make up your mind?''

Bobby looked up at his mother. He scrunched up his face. "I guess so.'' He tentatively took a bite. He didn't say anything, but continued to eat. She smiled when she saw a look on his face she knew well, the one that said he found something new that he liked.

She turned her attention to Shane, her manner business-like. "If you don't mind, I'd like to get myself a cup of coffee while Bobby eats his breakfast. We'll leave as soon as he's finished.''

Shane rose from his chair. "I'll get it for you.''

She maintained a standoffish attitude, as much for her own sake, in trying to keep her emotional equilibrium, as to send a message to him. "I don't want to inconvenience you.'' She stepped back into the den and started toward the kitchen, with Shane close behind her.

"Uh, about your leaving...''

His words cut through her outer show of control straight to her buried anxiety, triggering an angry reaction. She whirled to face him, speaking slowly as she carefully measured each word. "Don't worry. We'll be out of your house this morning just as I said we would. I've already packed our things.'' She glanced at the floor. "Except for these toys. I hadn't anticipated having breakfast here. I'd planned for us to be out of your house as soon as I got Bobby up.''

"I've, uh, been giving it some thought,'' Shane said.

She busied herself collecting Bobby's toys. "Whatever it is, I don't want to hear it. I'm not interested.''

He ignored her comments. "I don't know why Kate wanted you to stay here, but I've found that it's far easier to go along with what she wants than to try to fight her on anything.''

Cynthia turned a cool gaze on Shane, one that belied the nervous churning in her stomach. ''Well, you shouldn't have a problem with this one. You can tell Kate that I chose to leave.''

He awkwardly shifted his weight from one foot to the other and glanced at the floor. ''I guess I'm not making myself very clear.''

His nervousness and uncertainty caught her by surprise. They seemed completely out of character for the analytical, dynamic and confident Shane Fortune she used to know. This strange turn of events left her slightly perplexed. She thought everything had been settled last night. She wanted to move out of his house before things became more awkward than they already were. But mostly she wanted to get Bobby away from Shane. Protecting her son and his true identity was her number-one priority.

Shane cleared his throat as he took the toy police car from her hand, set the toy on the coffee table and then captured her wary gaze with his own. He fought the desire to reach out and touch her. He forged ahead, uncertain about where he was going. ''What I'm trying to say is that you can stay here—you and Bobby—until you settle your father's estate and find a place of your own. This is a large house. There's plenty of room for everyone. We don't have to feel crowded.''

He wasn't pleased with the expression on her face or her body language, which both said his logic hadn't convinced her. He offered a smile as he gestured toward the patio. ''And there's the swimming pool and hot tub.''

He saw her objections forming, but he adopted his most compelling bedside manner and continued before she had an opportunity to speak. ''I can imagine things have been very hectic for you the past couple of weeks. It's difficult enough to handle a long-distance move, and even more difficult to do it with a child.''

He glanced out the door of the den and could see Bobby still eating his breakfast. ''To add the emotional turmoil of your father's death to the circumstances is asking too much. The least I can do is allow you a safe and quiet haven in the middle of the chaos for a couple of weeks or so. You certainly can't take care of your business while living in a motel and trying to take care of your son, too. I'm at the hospital a good deal of the time, so you'd practically have the place to yourself.''

He held up his hand to prevent her from voicing her objections. ''Don't say anything now. Give it some thought while you have breakfast.'' He extended an engaging smile that he hoped would mask the uncertainty weaving its way through the fabric of his confidence. ''Okay?''

He saw her relent before the words came out of her mouth. ''I'll...I'll think about it.'' She turned her attention to picking up the rest of Bobby's toys.

Cynthia set the toy box on the coffee table next to the police car, then gazed out the door at Bobby. The little boy had taken his fire truck and was playing with it on the patio. She knew she could not conduct her business with her father's estate while keeping her son cooped up in a motel room all day. Even if she let him play outside, she certainly couldn't allow him to play in a parking lot or at the motel swimming pool without constant supervision.

She slowly turned to face Shane. She had reluctantly come to an uneasy decision. She made a valiant attempt to ignore the apprehension layered on top of her anxiety, caused as much by her unwanted attraction to Shane as by her all-important need to protect her secret.

He eyed her curiously. "Well?"

"I…" She stole another quick look at Bobby. Did she dare to stay in Shane's house and tempt fate? Trepidation shivered through her body. She shoved the words out quickly, before she could change her mind. "Yes. If it won't be too much of an imposition, we'll stay until I can get my father's estate straightened out."

"Well, that's settled then." An odd sensation washed over him. Whether or not he'd planned it, the fact remained that Cynthia McCree was back in his life. What he was not sure about was whether he had made the right decision and where that decision would lead. Intimate memories of their time together flooded through his mind, vividly bringing back desires and yearnings for what had once been.

"Yes, I guess it is. I suppose I should go upstairs and unpack our things." She stepped to the patio door and called to her son. "Come on, Bobby. Let's take your toys to your bedroom so they aren't cluttering up Shane's den, then you need to get dressed."

"In a minute, Mommy." He pushed the fire truck while making engine noises. "My firemen aren't done putting out the fire yet."

"I'll keep an eye on him if you want to go ahead and unpack."

She paused for a moment, not sure how to respond to Shane's offer. Even though she had started Bobby on swimming lessons at their neighborhood YMCA in Chicago, she didn't feel comfortable about leaving him alone by the swimming pool. But of even greater concern was leaving him alone with Shane. The last thing she needed was for Shane to question Bobby about where his father was. An uncomfortable lump knotted in the pit of her stomach and refused to go away. This was more than she had bargained for when she'd made the decision to move back to Pueblo. She had never figured close contact with Shane Fortune into the equation.

She watched her son playing with his truck. Her love for him flowed through her body, sending warmth to every corner of her existence. His innocence was balanced in a precarious position between the business she had to handle and her fear that Shane would discover his true identity. It was up to her to make sure that nothing—or no one— robbed him of his right to a happy childhood. She closed her eyes for a second and tried to still her rattled nerves. She had to be strong. She could not allow this temporary association with Shane to distract her.

Nor could she allow Shane to work his way into her heart again—a task she feared would not be all that difficult for him to achieve.

Cynthia stiffened her resolve. She had to make sure Shane didn't suspect that anything was amiss. "I'll only be gone for a few minutes. I'm sure Bobby won't need any attention other than someone just being here to make sure he doesn't try to go into the pool without supervision." She gave one last tentative glance in Bobby's direction and headed for the stairs.

Shane stood at the patio door watching Bobby play with his truck. Uncertainty welled up inside him—uncertainty about whether he had done the right thing, uncertainty about what the future held. An unidentified yet disturbing emotion pulled at his heartstrings. Bobby looked so much like Cynthia. Her son—a child who might have been theirs. His thoughts again wandered toward Bobby's father and what had happened to him. He watched Bobby until the emotional tug-of-war taking place inside him became more than he could handle.

He turned his attention toward the Native American artifacts Bobby had scattered on the floor. He began gathering them together. A small hand thrust a mask in front of his face.

"Here. I can help."

Bobby picked up a drum next and started to hand it to Shane, then paused. He looked at the drum, at Shane, then at the drum again. He hit it. A grin spread across his face and he hit it again. "I can be a Indian and you can be a cowboy."

An involuntary laugh escaped Shane's throat. "Maybe we should do that the other way around. Since I'm one-quarter Native American, I think you should be the cowboy, instead of me."

Bobby put down the drum. His eyes grew wide in amazement as he stared at Shane. "You're a real Indian?"

"I sure am. My grandmother's name was Natasha Lightfoot, and she was a full-blooded Papago. They've since changed the name to Tohono O'odham. There's a plateau with a sacred cave next to the reservation. Her family used to own the plateau and it's named for them."

"Do you know how to ride a horse? And shoot a bow and arrow?" The little boy's voice contained the same type of reverential awe often reserved for superheroes and sports stars.

"I sure do." Shane took in the fascination that covered Bobby's face. An odd sensation invaded his consciousness, a strange sort of tremor that started deep inside him and radiated throughout his body. He ventured a question, not sure exactly where he was going with it or even if he should ask it. "Would you like me to teach you how?" Another thought occurred to him, one that left him slightly unsettled. "If it's okay with your mother, that is." A surprising and unusual affinity with this little boy had been creeping up on him from the moment Bobby had turned around and asked him who he was early that morning. Was he starting something that couldn't be finished?

Bobby exuded excitement. "Yeah, I'd like that!"

"First we have to make sure it's okay with your mother," Shane repeated. He turned his attention to the items still on the floor. "But for now, let's finish putting these things back where they belong."

Shane placed the various items on the shelves, all but two. Bobby had held on to the drum and one of the Kachina dolls. Both were very old and valuable.

Bobby put the Kachina doll on the floor and turned his attention to the drum. Shane picked up the doll and carefully placed it on the coffee table. It was one of the few items he owned that had at one time actually belonged to his grandmother, a woman he never knew. She had died when his father was only eighteen.

What few possessions his grandmother had owned had finally been distributed among her grandchildren—his cousins, Jason and Tyler Fortune, his brother, Riley, and his sister Isabelle. The one possession that should have been his grandmother's was the one thing Shane wanted most—Lightfoot Plateau. The plateau and the cave were believed to have mystical powers. The Lightfoot family had been guardians of the plateau for centuries. One way or the other, he planned to have it back in the family.

Shane held up the Kachina doll. "Do you know what this is?"

Bobby took the doll from Shane's hand. He studied it, then made his pronouncement with all the authority of an expert testifying in court. "It's a Indian—a special one like the chief."

Shane smiled at Bobby. "That's very good, but he's even more special than that. This is a Kachina doll—"

"A *doll?*" Bobby scrunched up his nose. "Like girls play with?"

Shane suppressed a laugh. "No, more like your cowboy action figures. They're dolls."

Bobby's next words were almost a whisper, as if he didn't want Shane to hear them. "They aren't dolls. They're cowboys!"

Shane took the Kachina from Bobby, handling it carefully. His manner turned serious. "This isn't a play toy. A Kachina is a carved doll in a costume representing a spirit that has a special meaning for the tribe who believes in that spirit."

"It's not a toy? You can't play with them? What do you do with them?" The enthusiasm in Bobby's voice conveyed his fascination.

Shane tried to simplify the explanation so that Bobby would be able to understand. "The Native Americans who have the Kachinas believe that everything in the real world has a spirit that lives inside it. The Kachina dolls represent that spirit. The dolls depict men dressed in Kachina masks for special ceremonies where they call on the spirit of the Kachina." He paused for a moment as he ran his fingertips gently across the costumed figurine.

"The Kachina doll has a very special meaning for a tribe. This one belonged to my grandmother. It's usually given to a child as a gift. A friend of my grandmother was a Hopi. She gave the Hopi Kachina to my grandmother, who gave it to my father, and my father gave it to me."

Bobby's eyes grew wide with astonishment. "Gosh." He reached out and touched the Kachina, but did not try to take hold of it.

Cynthia stood at the door to the den taking in the scene

and the conversation between Shane and Bobby. It was a scene that should have warmed her heart—her son and his father enjoying a special moment together. But it didn't. Instead it sent a cold shiver through her body, followed by a surge of fear. She desperately wanted to put a stop to what she saw, but she couldn't do it without creating an awkward situation. Shane was obviously taken with Bobby, a reality that threatened her to the very core of her existence. And equally disturbing was the fascination Bobby seemed to have for Shane.

She blinked back the tears, trying to bring some calm to her shaken nerves and emotional turmoil, and entered the room. "I had the news on upstairs while I was unpacking. They announced a story on the construction of Fortune Memorial Children's Hospital in the next segment, right after the commercial." She turned on the television set, hoping the distraction would stop what she could plainly see was the beginning of a bonding between Bobby and Shane.

Shane was Bobby's father. Did she have the right to deny either of them that special father-and-son relationship? Or to deny her son that Native American part of his heritage that he seemed so fascinated with, something she'd noticed even before they'd left Chicago? She tried to shove the concerns aside, to tell herself there were far more important issues at stake. A twinge of guilt etched a path through her consciousness, taking up residence next to her anxiety. If only she had a clear-cut solution to her dilemma that would satisfy everyone's needs—one that would be *safe*.

Shane moved closer to the television, drawing her attention to the newscast. The scene was the construction site of the hospital, but the story was about something else.

It was a follow-up to a story about the construction foreman's accidental death being reclassified as murder.

The reporter went from that story to a segment about the Fortune Memorial Children's Hospital, which was followed by a taped interview with Dr. Shane Fortune in which he talked about the hospital project and then presented his concerns for the future of Lightfoot Plateau. Cynthia listened intently, taking in every word Shane said about the family's desire to give back to the community through the construction of the hospital.

When the segment concluded, Shane angrily snapped off the television. She could hear the disgust in his voice. "They certainly went out of their way to make sure the family name and the hospital project were thoroughly entwined with Mike Dodd's death. It was bad enough when his death in the elevator fall several months ago was thought to be an industrial accident at a Fortune Construction work site, but now that it's a murder case, they seem to be reveling in it. It's getting more and more difficult these days to find any difference between legitimate news and tabloid journalism."

Cynthia's brow furrowed. "I don't understand the public debate over Lightfoot Plateau. There seems to be a faction strongly in favor of preservation and another faction equally adamant in their desire to see the land developed." She turned to face Shane. "Isn't the land privately owned? Why would there be a public debate over it?"

"Yes, it's privately owned." His response carried the same note of displeasure she'd detected when he'd commented on the news story.

"I don't think I ever told you the story of the land. When my grandmother became pregnant by Ben Fortune, her family practically disowned her. Not only was she not married to Ben, he was still married to Kate Fortune and had no intention of getting a divorce. Natasha's family said she had disgraced them. They would not allow the land to stay in the Lightfoot family so that she would inherit it, especially when it meant that Ben Fortune might end up owning it.

"They sold Lightfoot Plateau to the Rowan family who still owns it. The land is adjacent to the hospital site and also borders the reservation. The Rowans have allowed the cave entrance to fall into disrepair, but their son, Brad, has agreed to return the plateau to the Fortunes when he marries my sister, Isabelle. Contrary to Brad's plans, I want to restore it and preserve the area as a place of historical significance for the various Native American tribes in this area."

She saw the determination in his features, the same type of dedication and all-out involvement in a cause she'd seen years ago. Once he made a commitment to something, nothing could deter him. A rush of sorrow caught her unprepared, tipping her delicately balanced emotions off center again. The sadness pushed at her reality. He had obviously never been committed to their relationship or to a shared future—certainly not the way she had been. She forced the upsetting thoughts from her mind and tried to shake off the disturbing feelings.

Cynthia glanced at Bobby. He was studying the pictures in a book he had taken from the shelf. If Shane had not been committed to their relationship, he would not have been committed to their son, either. Was she grasping at straws? Desperately searching for something to justify her decision to hide Bobby's true identity from him? She didn't think so, but that little shred of uncertainty still lingered at the back of her mind.

"Well—" Shane's voice broke into her thoughts "—I need to get going. I have a finance committee meeting for the Children's Hospital, then I need to do rounds at Pueblo General. I, uh, well, I have plans for this evening, so I won't be home for dinner.''

''That's quite all right.'' Had her words come out too quickly? She attempted to explain. ''I mean, I don't want our staying here to interfere with your usual routine.''

''I guess I'll see you later tonight.'' Shane hurried out of the den and up the stairs to his bedroom.

It had been an odd interlude and it left him unnerved, although he wasn't sure exactly why. The conversation had turned to a topic that did not involve dredging up moments from their past union. Yet a tingling undercurrent of heated desire continued to race through his body. His breathing quickened and his pulse jumped.

He didn't have any plans for that evening. He wasn't even sure why he said he had. The only thing he was certain of was his need to get out of that room. The walls had started to close in around him. He needed to go someplace where he could think without the very real distraction presented by Cynthia McCree's presence.

The undeniably disconcerting affect she had on his senses left him as much bewildered as it did longing to renew their affair. It was an idea that had often crossed his mind and inflamed his desires, but it had been safely tucked away as something that could never be. He had never gotten her out of his system, but he thought he had reconciled himself to the fact that she was no longer part of his life. Then when he'd found her in his house in the middle of the night, everything had come rushing back at him. She had changed a great deal over the past six years. She was every bit as desirable, but now it was combined with a new maturity and confidence.

There was also her son and the unanswered questions

about the little boy's father. And there was that empty feeling inside him that had never gone away.

He dressed quickly for work, then hurried downstairs. He paused at the bottom of the staircase and glanced at Cynthia in the den. His heartbeat picked up again. Everything meshed together in one baffling tableau of what had been, what was now and what could be. It left him utterly bewildered.

He turned away. There was no need to have any further conversation with Cynthia before he left for work. He went through the kitchen and into the garage, then tried to collect his thoughts as he drove to the hospital. He needed to talk to Kate. He could not imagine why she'd offered the use of his house to Cynthia.

He had even gone so far as to compound a tenuous situation by insisting that she stay until she could get her business matters settled. He wasn't sure what had prompted him to do that, and it had probably been a really bad idea. But was it one he would live to regret?

Three

———

"What's the matter, Mommy?" Bobby asked worriedly as he placed his fire truck on the patio table in front of her.

Cynthia opened her eyes. "It's nothing, honey." Bad enough that her decision to keep Bobby's identity from Shanc had already laid a heavy dose of guilt on her. Now she'd compounded that guilt by allowing her son to see her weakness and despair. "Mommy just has a bit of a headache, that's all."

"Why does your head ache? Did you hurt it?"

She couldn't resist grinning as she wrapped her arms around her son and gave him a loving squeeze. No matter how bleak things seemed or how distraught she felt, all she had to do was hug Bobby and the world suddenly became a brighter place. "I guess I did. I hurt it by thinking too much about your grandpa's belongings. Taking care of his things is going to take more time than I thought."

She had spent the day working on her father's estate. She had gathered his papers and business effects from his apartment, along with items of sentimental value. There was nothing else there that warranted the effort or expense of putting it into storage. She made arrangements to have the apartment cleaned out and the remaining items disposed of.

That left only the task of sorting out the tangled mess of her father's estate. She had been shocked by the poverty-stricken appearance of his living conditions, yet the paperwork told a different story. What she'd thought would be a straightforward situation had turned into a time-consuming nightmare.

"Does that mean we can stay here longer?"

She looked at the eager expression on his face. "I…I don't know. We'll have to see what happens."

"I like it here. Shane has neat stuff. He let me play his drum."

She had to admit it had been a real blessing to have Shane's house as her base of operation rather than a motel room. Bobby had been bored and fidgety while they were at her father's apartment that morning, but as soon as they returned to Shane's where he had his toys, the patio, the yard and the pool, he'd been content.

She broached the subject carefully, not wanting to suggest anything by her voice other than the meaning of her words. "You need to be very careful when you handle Shane's things. They aren't toys, and if one of them gets broken, it will cost a lot of money to replace it. Some of them are very old and can't even be replaced."

"I'll be careful. Shane told me about the dolls, only they aren't like dolls that girls play with. One of them belonged to his grandma. He let me hold it."

Bobby's fascination with all things Native American

was yet another concern, one tied in with her uneasiness about her decision to keep his true identity hidden from Shane. Native American culture was part of his heritage, something he should know about. Would she be able to effectively introduce him to it without Shane's becoming involved? She tried to shake away the negative thoughts and dwell more on the positive ones. Now that they were back in Pueblo, there were numerous places and ways to acquaint him with his heritage. As soon as everything was wrapped up and she had them settled in their own house, she would make that her number-one priority.

Bobby turned toward the pool. ''I want to go in the water.''

She smiled at him while smoothing back his hair with her hand. ''Tell you what. You pick up your toys and put them away in your room while I change into my swimsuit, and then we'll both go into the water.'' She stood up and quickly stacked all the papers she'd been working with into a file box and closed the lid.

She frowned as she glanced at her watch, then turned her attention back to Bobby. ''It's later than I thought, a little after five-thirty. I think it's time to get ready for dinner. Aren't you hungry?''

''No, I'm not hungry—honest. Can't we go in the pool? Please, Mommy?''

She saw his disappointment. Knowing how much he loved the water, she relented. ''How about this? You put your toys away and I'll start dinner. Then while it's cooking, we can go in the pool for a little bit. Okay?''

He grinned. ''Okay.'' He began gathering up his toys.

Cynthia went to the kitchen and took several items from the refrigerator. They had been eating all their meals in restaurants ever since they'd arrived in Pueblo. She looked forward to having a leisurely meal she'd prepared herself.

Shane had said he wouldn't be home for dinner, so there would be just the two of them. She'd stopped at the grocery store on their way back from her father's apartment and purchased some groceries. She quickly mixed a meat loaf and scrubbed a couple of potatoes, then put everything in the oven to bake. She would fix a salad and another vegetable in about an hour when it was time for them to eat.

With that handled, she went to see how Bobby was doing. "You need to take your toys to your room. I'll help you carry them upstairs, then you can put them away while I change into my swimsuit."

Ten minutes later they were in the pool. Cynthia called to Bobby from the deep end. "Okay. I'm ready." The invigorating water washed over her skin, refreshing her lagging spirits and reviving her tired disposition. It was just the pick-me-up she needed to get her out of her despondent state of mind.

She treaded water and watched as Bobby enthusiastically ventured out to the end of the diving board. He waved to her, then jumped into the deep water. He kicked his way back up to the surface. As soon as he popped up, she was right there to give him any help he needed. She stayed at his side as he dog-paddled his way to the edge of the pool.

She marveled every time he took that fearless leap into the deep water. He had absolute trust in her. He *knew* she would always be there to help him. Even though she tried, she couldn't stop her thoughts from wandering back to a time when she'd trusted Shane completely and totally. She'd believed he would never do anything to hurt her. It had been a long time ago, a lesson painfully learned. Those memories used to trigger instant anger. Now they brought sadness and distress.

She called to Bobby, who'd climbed onto the diving board again, ready to go. "Do you think you can jump all the way out to where I am?" She'd swum away a few feet. She hoped her son would never lose that ability to trust, that no one would ever take it away from.

"Bombs away!" Bobby shouted, then laughed as he ran the length of the diving board and leapt off the end, making as big a splash as a five-year-old could.

The sounds from the pool carried into the house. Shane stood in the den just inside the sliding door to the patio. He watched Cynthia and Bobby. It was enticing, coming home and finding the house full of laughter and play, rather than silence.

His life was busy and fulfilling. He had long ago made peace with his dual heritage and carved out his place in the world. He had established a successful career as a doctor. He found his volunteer work at the Native American Center rewarding. Twice a month he volunteered doing medical rounds on the reservation.

But no matter how much he did, how many projects he took on, it was not enough to fill the emptiness that lived inside him. It usually caught up with him late at night when he was alone, at a time when he reflected on his life choices and what it might have been like if he had made different choices. Every time he took on another cause, he thought it would be the one to drive away that emptiness, but each time the empty feeling and the loneliness that went with it worked its way back into his reality.

It had finally gotten to the point where he knew he had too many things going on in his life. There was no way he could give a full commitment to any new endeavors. And still he felt empty. Whatever doubts he had about the future were private thoughts, which he did not share with anyone. They remained hidden behind the facade of the Shane Fortune everyone *thought* they knew.

Now, hearing and seeing Cynthia and Bobby cavorting in his pool, a warmth invaded his uncertainties, but was quickly replaced by sadness. He may have reconciled himself to where and how he fit into the world, but he didn't know how Cynthia would be able to straddle his dual existence now any more than he did back then. That knowledge did not keep the heated desire she'd stirred from continuing to plague him, though—desire that swept through his body like a raging fire each time he saw her.

And then there was her son. The emotion overwhelmed him and he had to turn away. The appealing family scene pulled too heavily on his heartstrings and produced uninvited thoughts of what might have been. He truly wanted to be a part of the type of closeness he'd just witnessed, but it was an area he was not yet emotionally prepared to explore.

The aroma of cooking food drew him to the kitchen. He paused to open a bottle of wine and pour himself a glass before looking in the oven. Only two baked potatoes. He checked the refrigerator and noted that she had purchased some groceries. He leaned back against the counter and took a sip of his wine. He had told her he wouldn't be home for dinner, and she obviously wasn't expecting him. He wasn't sure, exactly, why he had come home. He had called his brother to see if they could have dinner together, but Riley already had other plans. He didn't have anywhere else to go, so he came home to what had always been an empty house.

He took his glass and carried it out to the patio. Cynthia and Bobby had moved to the shallow end of the pool. Even though it was obviously play time, she was mixing it with swimming instructions. Bobby clearly loved the water and showed no fear. He was just the kind of boy any man would be proud to call his son. He wondered if that applied to Bobby's father, too.

As for Cynthia…no woman had even come close to measuring up to her in his mind or in his heart. He had compared every woman he had ever been with to Cynthia, and all of them had come up short. He knew he wanted her back in his life, but what he didn't know was how much he was willing or able to give. He continued to sip his wine while watching Cynthia and Bobby. He tried to put a stop to his wandering thoughts and escalating yearnings, but to no avail.

"Okay, one more time, then we need to get out of the water. Let's see you swim to the side of the pool." Cynthia moved away from Bobby and watched as he splashed his way through the water. The move back to Pueblo would be good for her son, just as she'd hoped. A swimming pool was definitely a must on her list when she looked for a house for the two of them.

Bobby climbed up the steps leading out of the pool. His face lit up as he glanced toward the house. "Did you see me, Shane? Did you see me swim?"

Bobby's words brought her to a halt halfway up the steps. Cynthia turned toward the house and saw Shane standing there watching them. A nervous jitter started up, quickly combining with the trepidation that had been just below the surface from the moment she'd discovered it was Shane's house.

He told her he would not be home until later tonight. She had thought she would be *safe* from his tempting presence and magnetic sex appeal. She climbed the rest of the steps out of the water, grabbed a large towel from the chair, then handed a second towel to Bobby. "Dry yourself off properly before going inside." She glanced at Shane, then back to her son. "Be careful that you don't drip water in the house, okay?"

He took the towel from her. "Okay, Mommy."

He darted over to Shane, dragging the towel along the ground behind him. He grinned from ear to ear. "Did you see me swim? Did I do good?"

The little boy's excitement was infectious. "I sure did, champ. You looked real good."

Shane swung his gaze to Cynthia. She had one foot on the edge of the lounge chair as she patted the water from her leg. He visually caressed every curve of her body, the image of which had remained burned into his memory for six years. *And you look better than good. You look absolutely delicious.* He didn't even try to censor the errant thought. He allowed it to settle inside him, touching every corner of his being with warmth and sensual longing.

As soon as Cynthia finished drying herself, she took the towel and headed after Bobby, catching up with him where he'd stopped to talk to Shane. She dried his back. "You have just enough time before dinner to take your bath and get into your pajamas."

"Aw, Mommy…" He squirmed out of her hold. "I can't put my pajamas on *before* dinner. It's too early. That's for babies." He looked up at Shane, obviously seeking his support. "Isn't that right, Shane? Only babies go to bed this early."

Cynthia leveled a look at Shane that said his interference was not welcome. He quickly raised his hands in surrender, took a step back and let out an amused chuckle as he surveyed the expectant look on Bobby's face. "Whoa. I can't help you there, champ. I'm afraid you're going to have to negotiate that one with your mother."

She wrapped the towel around Bobby's shoulders. "You forgot that it's much later than we usually eat dinner. You don't have to go to bed right away, but you'll be ready. Now, upstairs with you.''

Bobby was not happy, but did as instructed. He hung his head, then pulled the towel from his shoulders and trailed it along the floor behind him as he headed toward the stairs.

''That's quite a boy you have there. You've done a good job of raising him—'' Shane paused, not sure of exactly how to phrase his comment ''—all by yourself.''

It was more a question than a statement, and it left her very uneasy. The air suddenly seemed much cooler and a chill darted across her skin. Did he suspect? Was he probing for information, or was it just an innocent comment? She finally managed to mumble, ''Yes, Bobby is a marvelous boy. He's the most important thing in my life.''

Anxiety swamped her. The awkward moment left her vulnerable and very much aware that she was dressed in only a two-piece swimsuit that suddenly felt much skimpier than it actually was. She looked up at Shane. There was no mistaking the way his gaze raked her body. A moment later their gazes met. She could not ignore the heat that burned in the depth of his dark eyes. Nor could she ignore the incendiary desire that scorched the very depths of her existence.

''I…I need to change into some dry clothes.'' She knew what she really needed to do was get away from Shane Fortune. She started for the door into the den, then paused and turned. The way he was looking at her sent a shiver of desire through her. The emotional threat struck at the very core of her life. She could not allow herself to be taken in by his considerable charm and sex appeal.

She forced a businesslike attitude in an attempt to cover any emotions that might have seeped through. ''You said you wouldn't be here for dinner, so I'm afraid I only fixed enough for Bobby and me.''

''I noticed that you bought groceries,'' he said. ''You didn't need to do that. There's plenty of food here, more than enough for everyone.''

''I can afford to take care of my son and myself. I don't want to impose on your, uh, generosity any more than we already have. It didn't seem right for us to eat your food, especially when you said you weren't going to be here.''

''I…'' He followed her into the den. His words came out like a soft caress, exposing some of the feelings coursing through his veins. ''My meeting was canceled.''

''I see.'' She forced out the words, but knew it was an incredibly inadequate response. She hurried toward the stairs, afraid to look back for fear that she might expose too much of what was going on inside her.

Shane watched her until she disappeared around the corner. Once again the bands tightened across his chest and the heat settled low in his body. More than anything he wanted to touch her, to hold her.

He busied himself in the kitchen while Cynthia and Bobby were changing. By the time she returned, Shane had set the table, made a salad and put a potato in the microwave for himself.

''It looks to me as if you have enough meat loaf for all of us.'' He cocked his head as he leveled a questioning gaze in her direction, paying particular attention to the obvious nervousness that covered her like a blanket. ''Do you mind if I join you for dinner?''

''Of course not.'' Cynthia avoided making eye contact with him, busying herself by grabbing a package of mixed vegetables from the freezer. She forced a casual tone into her words, even though it was far removed from what she felt. ''After all, it is your house.'' She had not anticipated a quiet little dinner for three. Her gaze darted around the kitchen as her mind searched for something to add an impersonal touch to the setting. Then she found it.

"I hope it's not too late to catch the news." She turned on the small television that sat at the end of the counter. The newscast was filled with local stories, chief among them the Mike Dodd murder case. The Fortune name was again prominently featured. She noticed the displeasure on Shane's face and the way his jaw tightened as he watched the report.

"It's bad enough that they have to keep dragging the family name through the mud, but doing all their reports as live remotes with the Children's Hospital in the background is going too far. There's no purpose served by constantly linking the hospital construction with the murder as if they were two halves of the same whole."

His words were precise and his manner totally controlled, but she could read between the lines. She knew the tension that lived behind that calm facade. "Is there anything you can do to make them change the tone of their reporting?"

A hard look of determination crossed his face. "I talked to the news director today about their less-than-professional handling of this story. I offered to go to the station and do a televised interview about the hospital project, its benefit to the community and what it means for the various Native American tribes in the area, in hopes I could shift the emphasis of their broadcast. I thought I would hear back this afternoon, but so far there hasn't been any word from him."

She had seen his devotion to the hospital project and heard it in his voice. She knew that his stubborn nature would not allow him to abandon something once he'd made a commitment. It was the same type of passion he'd displayed when he'd told her about his determination to get Lightfoot Plateau away from the Rowan family.

The three of them sat down at the table and ate dinner. Bobby seemed oblivious to any tension in the air, but Cynthia was aware—and very concerned. Bobby was a perceptive child with a healthy curiosity. She didn't want her son—*their son*—to start asking questions about Shane and her. She made an attempt to lighten the atmosphere by engaging in small talk.

"The, uh, hospital—Pueblo General—certainly took good care of my father. They even provided some daycare facilities in the afternoon where Bobby could play." She smoothed back Bobby's hair where it draped over his forehead in an unruly manner. A smile curved her mouth as the love she felt for her son welled up inside her. "It was really a blessing for me. I felt terrible about Bobby being cooped up in Daddy's hospital room all day."

She nervously cleared her throat and quickly returned to a more businesslike manner. "I was very impressed with the hospital staff. They seemed to be quite efficient."

"You should have come by my office at the hospital. I would have been glad to keep an eye on Bobby."

"That certainly wasn't necessary. Besides, I'm sure you had far too much work to do...seeing patients, making rounds, things like that." She rose from her chair and began clearing dishes from the table and placing them on the counter by the sink.

Bobby looked up from his dinner and stared at Shane for a moment. "Do you work at the hospital?"

"I sure do. I'm a doctor."

"Did you take care of my grandpa?"

Shane saw the openness on Bobby's face. "No, I didn't."

"Why? Don't you like my grandpa?"

A sharp twinge caused Shane a moment's discomfort. He had never been friends with Robert McCree, a fact that had been driven home when Cynthia's father refused to tell him where she had gone. No matter what their personal relationship, however, it wouldn't have prevented him from doing all he could as a doctor if he'd known her father was in the hospital.

He regarded Bobby, who was quietly waiting for an answer to his question. "The hospital is a very large and busy place, Bobby. I didn't know your grandfather was there."

He shot a quick glance at Cynthia. "If your mother had told me, I certainly would have looked in on him and made sure…" His voice trailed off. He didn't know where he was going with his comments. He would have looked in on Robert McCree and made sure…what? That he would have gotten well? That he wouldn't have died? Shane didn't know exactly what to say to the little boy, so he ended up not finishing his sentence.

Cynthia stepped into the awkward lull. "Shane already had lots of patients of his own to take care of. Your grandfather had a different doctor taking care of him."

Bobby looked at Shane, then at his mother. "Oh."

She extended a confident smile toward Bobby. "Finish your vegetables. We have some ice cream for dessert."

Bobby returned to his dinner while Cynthia resumed her clean-up activities by putting the dirty dishes in the dishwasher. A moment later Shane rearranged everything she'd put in the dishwasher. She put things away, and again he rearranged her work, putting everything in a different place.

An exasperated Cynthia had all she could stand of Shane's silent disapproval and apparent criticism. She whirled around to confront him. "Would you prefer that I leave everything sitting out so you can put them away yourself?'' She couldn't keep the sarcasm out of her voice. ''That way you can make sure it's done *properly*.''

She could not handle any more of the stress that had been piling up on her shoulders ever since she'd received the phone call about her father being taken to the hospital. All the pent-up anxieties and pressures of the past couple of weeks exploded inside her. She knew she had to get away from everyone before she said something she'd regret. She hurried out of the kitchen and through the den. She opened the sliding glass door, stepped out onto the patio and took a deep breath.

An almost uncontrollable tremor shivered through her body, followed by a sick churning of fear that settled in the pit of her stomach. Staying in Shane's house was not going to work, not even for a few days—let alone a couple of weeks. She squeezed her eyes shut. She couldn't keep up the pretense of indifference. She had tried, but it just wasn't working. She had probably overreacted to Shane's behavior in the kitchen. He hadn't really done anything that was so terrible. She stared at the shimmering water in the pool and wondered what to do.

Her body stiffened. A jolt of panic raced through her, leaving her momentarily unnerved. She'd left Bobby in the kitchen with Shane—the two of them alone together. She hurried back into the house just as Shane entered the den from the hallway. She felt a wave of relief, but it was tempered by the expression on his face.

''What's the matter with you, Cynthia?''

She heard the annoyance in his voice. It didn't surprise her, although his expression was one of concern more than anything else. She tried to remain standoffish. She battled the nearly overwhelming need to have him touch her… hold her…kiss her. She desperately wanted the comfort and security she had at one time associated with being wrapped in his embrace. But it was not to be. She was so frightened and felt so very alone. She managed to control the butterflies flitting around in her stomach. "I…I don't know what you mean."

"Why did you almost snap my head off back there in the kitchen? I understand that you're upset about your father, but I'm not the one who brought up the subject of the hospital and the time he was there."

His words caught her by surprise. They weren't at all what she'd expected to hear. She stared at him for a moment as she tried to collect her thoughts. He didn't seem to have a clue what he'd done. Perhaps it wasn't intentional and she really had overreacted. Then she saw him frown as he bent down to pick up a couple of Bobby's blocks from under the coffee table. A jab of irritation kicked her anger into gear again.

She took the blocks from his hand. "Little boys aren't neat and tidy, and apparently I don't keep things in my kitchen in the same places you keep yours in your kitchen. When I agreed to stay here, it was because you said you were hardly ever home, that we wouldn't be in each other's way. It seems obvious to me that I'm in your way. This arrangement isn't working out."

She turned away from him. "Perhaps it would be better if Bobby and I were to check into a motel, after all, so your routine won't be disturbed." Her words contained a bit of an edge even though they were meant more for herself than him.

His hand came down on her arm and he turned her toward him. She stared at the floor, afraid to meet his gaze. Then he grasped her shoulders, which sent a surge of excitement rippling across her skin. His voice enveloped her like a warm embrace. Anything he said at that moment would sound as soft as a sensual caress. ''You know that's not practical. Nor is it fair to Bobby.''

He pulled her closer. His breath tickled her cheek. Then he enclosed her in his arms, holding her body tightly against his. His heartbeat resonated in her, conveying his strength and filling her with a sense of safety and well-being. It felt so good being in his arms again. For a brief moment she was transported back to a time when her life was simple and she had no worries. If only she could figure out how to make time stand still so the feeling could last forever.

A flash of reality quickly brought her back into focus. She could not allow any type of intimacy between Shane and herself, regardless of the tingling warmth rushing through her veins now. It was far too risky. She shoved back from him. Her primary concern was to protect her son and guard his identity. That had to come before anything else.

She put as much conviction into her voice as she could muster, all the while fighting down the trepidation that tried to work its way to the open. ''We've been down this road before, Shane. Let's not travel it again. I've done a lot of growing up since I last saw you. I can take care of myself—and my son.''

She hurried back to the kitchen and away from Shane. She took a calming breath in an attempt to rid herself of the highly charged combination of excitement and apprehension coursing through her body—both caused by her physical contact with Shane. But it didn't help to pacify her nearly unmanageable emotions that were running amok as a result of their physical contact. And the most frightening aspect was that it had all happened so quickly—and so easily. One moment she was alone and the next she was in his arms, allowing his strength and sensual warmth to flow through her.

She turned her attention to Bobby, fixing him with a loving smile that she hoped covered the out-of-control anxiety rampaging through her body. "Have you finished your dinner?"

"Yeah, I finished everything." Bobby grinned from ear to ear as he held up his plate to show her. He looked at her expectantly. "Can I have my ice cream now?"

"You sure can." She scooped some chocolate ice cream into a bowl and set it on the table in front of him. Then she carried his plate to the sink. That's when she noticed it. He had tried to throw away some of his vegetables, rather than eating all of them. She started to say something, then changed her mind. Grinning, she realized that she had done the same thing when she was his age. But as she rinsed off the plate and put it in the dishwasher, a shiver darted across the back of her neck, and her breath caught in her throat. She didn't need to turn around to know what had caused it. Instinctively she knew Shane was standing in the doorway watching her. She felt his eyes on her, a sensation that left her very unnerved.

Four

——

This was definitely a different woman from the one he had known before, Shane thought as he leaned against the doorjamb and watched as Cynthia dished up Bobby's ice cream. The tightness pulled across his chest, leaving him decidedly unsettled. Just looking at her sent a charge of desire through his body the same way it always had, but now there was more.

For perhaps the first time he consciously looked past the beautiful face, the creamy skin and the sensuality that had, in the past, soothed him after a weary day. This was an independent assertive woman who was not afraid to speak her mind. This was a new dimension to her character, one he found very appealing. It was also something that would be the cause of continued conflict between them unless he could find some sort of neutral ground.

His life had been running smoothly. He had problems to deal with, but he knew what he was doing and what he needed to do. Her arrival had turned his entire world upside down. Even just the thought of her made his pulse race and his breathing difficult. He tried to make some sense of his escalating bewilderment, but his confusion ran unchecked. He had come to the realization long ago that he'd made a huge mistake when he'd terminated his relationship with Cynthia McCree. And now she had a son. A son who should have been his.

It was a thought that continued to jar his reality. Bobby was a terrific little boy. Every time he thought about what could have been, it tore him up inside.

He also had another dynamic to consider, another problem to try to work through. Before he could hope to establish any type of relationship with Cynthia, he needed to work hard to win her back. It was a matter of trust, something he had destroyed between them six years ago. He also knew there could be no type of a relationship with her without a firmly established relationship with Bobby.

He drew in a steadying breath and stepped into the kitchen. His light and easy outer attitude hid the uncertainty churning inside him. He extended a questioning smile. "Do you have any more ice cream there for someone else who ate all his vegetables?" She looked up. He saw the wariness in her eyes but wasn't sure what it meant.

"I suppose so." She dished up another scoop of ice cream and handed the bowl to him without further comment.

Shane ate the ice cream while watching Cynthia as she finished cleaning the kitchen. "That was a good dinner, Cynthia."

"Thank you."

Her words sounded as frosty as his ice cream tasted. Was it just his imagination? She seemed to be avoiding any personal contact, even something as simple as looking directly at him. He pushed on, determined to make some sort of small talk with her, if nothing else.

"It's sort of a nuisance to cook for only one person. I usually end up with something from the freezer that I can pop into the microwave, or I eat out. It was nice having a truly home-cooked meal for a change."

When she didn't respond, he carried his empty bowl to the sink and tried another topic of conversation, one where she would have to say something. "How are things coming with your father's estate? Is there anything I can do to help?"

Her entire body seemed to go slack as if she could no longer maintain her stiff posture. She emitted a sigh of despair and leaned back against the counter. Her voice carried a weariness. "It's not going well at all. I can't believe what a mess it is. Even the things that are obvious are a convoluted disaster from a legal standpoint. So far, it's been a real nightmare."

"What's the problem? Is there something I can help with?"

"A lot of it is the technicality of making everything consistent. It seems that he kept signing documents using variations of his name. Sometimes he'd use only his first and last name, other times it was his first name and middle initial, and on other documents he used his first name and full middle name. It wouldn't have been so bad if he'd been consistent within the confines of a transaction.

"On his car, for example, he has his signature one way on the title, another way on the registration and yet another way on the bank loan for the car. It's going to be a matter of obtaining a legal document stating that all three signatures are the same person and then having to deal individually with all entities involved. It's that way on just about everything he owns—car, bank accounts, deeds to land.

And to complicate things even more, there're notations about a couple of safe-deposit boxes and one safe-deposit box key, but there's no readily available information about where these boxes are located."

Again she could not stop a little sigh of despair. "I'm afraid it's going to mean a lot of standing in lines at various windows and going through state and county records, plus numerous phone calls to even determine what he owns and what he no longer owns before I can even start straightening out the signature problem."

A sob caught in her throat as she blinked away a tear. She had been fighting the emotion surrounding her father's death while battling the tangle of his estate. That, combined with the unexpected upheaval of being thrown back together with Shane, had started to take its toll. She wanted so much to be strong and project a calm control while keeping the real state of her nerves hidden, but it was a losing battle.

She tried one last time to pull herself together. "He was living in a pigsty of an apartment in near-poverty conditions, yet he owns real estate and has several bank accounts."

Cynthia finally looked up at Shane, her features contorted into a mask of anger and disbelief. He saw her fight back the tears, but she could not hold back the rush of angry words. "How could he do this to me? How could he have allowed his entire life to become such a mess and then leave it to me to fix?"

"Mommy? Are you mad at Grandpa?"

The shock of Bobby's question brought her up short. She hadn't realized he was listening to her. She knelt next to him and carefully measured her words, making sure no hint of anger crept into her voice. "No, of course not. I'm not mad at Grandpa."

"You sounded mad. Did Grandpa do something bad?"

She hugged Bobby to her as she fought back another tear. She struggled to get her emotional outburst under control. "No, honey, Grandpa didn't do anything bad." She closed her eyes and took a calming breath, silently berating herself for allowing her emotions to show in front of Bobby.

She stood up and took Bobby's hand. "It's getting late. Almost your bedtime. Why don't you go up to your room and pick out a book we can read together? While you're doing that, I'll put the rest of these dishes in the dishwasher, then I'll be right up." She gave him an encouraging smile. "Okay?"

"Can Shane come to bed with us, too? We can all read a story."

She nearly choked on Bobby's unexpected question. It took her a few seconds to regain her breath. She scrambled to come up with an appropriate reply. "Uh, well, I think Shane has other things he needs to do right now. You run up and pick out a book, and I'll be up in a couple of minutes." She watched as he climbed the stairs to the second floor.

She knew her face was flushed a bright crimson. She didn't dare look at Shane. She busied herself with little chores. Then, without looking in Shane's direction, she hurried toward the kitchen door.

Shane grabbed her arm, bringing her to a halt. A soft chuckle accompanied his words. "Kids say the darnedest things, don't they?"

She maneuvered her arm out of his grasp as she turned to face him. "It was the innocent remark of a child, nothing more. Certainly not an invitation." Once again memories of passion-filled nights flooded her mind. "You've apparently made quite an impression on him."

He again saw the wariness in her eyes and felt the tension in her body. He immediately dropped any attempt to make light of what Bobby had said and returned to their previous topic of conversation. "It sounds as if your father's estate is going to be a lot more work and take more time than you originally anticipated."

"Yes—"

He stopped her before she said anything else. She had to stay, and it was up to him to convince her. "Which is all the more reason for you and Bobby to stay here until you have everything straightened out. It's certainly more comfortable for you than a motel would be. You'll have a quiet place to take care of your business. You won't have a motel charging you an outrageous fee for every phone call you make. And as far as Bobby is concerned, you know he'll be much safer here in a gated community than at a motel where strangers are constantly coming and going."

His manner softened as he took her hand. Her muscles tensed, but she didn't pull away. "I can imagine how hard this must be for you," he said. "It's stressful enough to pack up your life and move across the country to start over, even more stressful when you do it with a child. And then losing a parent on top of that and having to deal with the nightmare of his estate. The very least I can do is supply you with a safe and tranquil place to pull yourself together and take care of your business. In fact, I insist. This is probably what Kate had in mind when she sent you here."

She studied him for a moment. She could see the honesty and sincerity on his face and hear it in his voice. When she set aside her personal concerns and viewed the situation in an unbiased light, she knew he was right. Somehow she had to bear up under the stress of a daily association with a man who could rip her life apart if he ever learned the truth about Bobby. She prayed she had the strength to handle it, but had never felt as unsure about anything in her life.

She nervously cleared her throat, then rushed her words while she still had the ability to get them out. "You're right. It does make sense—for the time being." She renewed her determination. "But as soon as the estate stuff is done, I'll be looking for a job and a house of my own. Hopefully we won't be in your way very long."

His voice was soft, his words genuine. "You're welcome for as long as it takes."

It was a quiet moment as they stood in the kitchen, Shane continuing to clasp her hand in his. Cynthia allowed the physical contact, taking delight in the sensual pleasure that flowed from his touch. It was as if a truce had been signed and some of the friction resolved. The moment was one of intimate softness that stirred up equally intimate memories and desires.

A somewhat flustered Cynthia finally broke the silence. "I...I'd better get upstairs. Bobby is expecting a story."

"As soon as you're done, I have some things I want to discuss with you. Perhaps you'll join me for a glass of wine?"

She finally slipped her hand out of his. Her words were almost a whisper as if she was afraid to say them. "If you'd like."

Shane watched as she climbed the stairs, then he opened a bottle of wine and retrieved two glasses from the cupboard. It was a nice evening so he carried everything out to the patio. There had been a time when he believed he knew everything she thought and everything she felt. He had not allowed the idea that she might be as strong a woman as the one he'd seen since he'd found her in his house a couple of nights ago—strong, independent and determined. They were qualities that suited her well. They had transformed a beautiful woman who had driven his senses wild into someone even more desirable.

He poured himself a glass of wine, then leaned back in his chair and stared at the swimming pool. The underwater lights caused the water to shimmer brightly in the surrounding darkness. He didn't fight the thoughts that circulated through his mind. He wanted to help her, but more importantly he wanted her back in his life. It was not going to be easy. He needed to be cautious so he didn't end up doing something he might regret. The truth was, he didn't know exactly what he wanted. He hadn't been this confused since he'd tried to justify his deplorable actions of six years ago when he cut Cynthia McCree out of his life.

And lurking in the back of his mind, but never far away from his primary thoughts, was her son. There had been a couple of times when he could have questioned Bobby about his father—when he'd *wanted* to ask him some questions—but had decided against it at the last moment. He wasn't even sure why. Perhaps he was afraid to find out what had happened. Perhaps he didn't want to dredge up the very real possibility that he was responsible for driving her directly into the arms of a man who had treated her badly, then deserted her in her time of need.

If that was what had happened. A tremor made its way through his body, then settled in his stomach as an uncomfortable churning. There was another notion about Bobby's parentage swirling around even further in the back of his mind. It had not crystallized into a solid thought, at least not yet, but the very essence left him troubled and unsettled. He took a sip of his wine in an effort to calm his jangled nerves.

Cynthia's return interrupted his wandering thoughts before they went too far astray and ended up someplace he wasn't ready to go. He poured her a glass of wine. She took it, then seated herself across the table from him.

"Bobby went right to sleep. I think he really wore himself out in the pool today."

"He sure seems to like the water."

"He loves it. Living here will really be good for him." The unintentional implication of her words produced an awkward pause. She felt the heated flush of embarrassment spread across her cheeks again. "I didn't mean living *here*. I meant, our moving to Pueblo would allow him to be outdoors and have access to a swimming pool year-round, other than the one at the YMCA." An amused twinkle darted through his eyes. She didn't know whether to be irritated with him for making fun of her or embarrassed by what she had said.

"What made you decide to move back to Pueblo? Was it your father's health?"

"No, I had already given notice at my job and was packing when I found out he'd been taken to the hospital." Her brow furrowed as some of her earlier anger shot through her again. "If only he'd told me…if only I'd known he was in bad health, then maybe…if I'd been here, instead of Chicago, I could have straightened out…"

She shook her head while staring down at her wineglass. Her voice was soft, her words hesitant. "I'm sorry. I shouldn't have gotten angry like that, and earlier, in front of Bobby…I can't imagine what prompted me to say those things."

She looked up, making fleeting eye contact with Shane before turning her gaze away. "I must have sounded horrible, taking my frustrations out on my father like that."

"It's perfectly natural, you know. Anger is one of the steps in the grieving process."

She looked out across the swimming pool, took several

deep breaths to calm her nerves, then stared at her glass again. Her audible sigh only served to reinforce the despair that filled her voice. "If only he'd told me he was in bad health. I called him a couple of times every month just to talk and he spent every Christmas since I left Pueblo at my house, but he never mentioned any health problems. Just last month we discussed my decision to move back to Pueblo and he never said…"

Shane reached across the table and placed his hand on top of hers, initiating the physical contact he'd longed for from the moment she had returned to the patio. The feel of her skin sent a warm surge up his arm and through his body that confirmed what he already knew. He wanted much more of her—he wanted all of her. But he knew before anything else could happen that he needed to repair the damage he'd done when he'd left her.

So for now he contented himself with providing the emotional comfort and support she obviously needed. "It's important for you to allow the anger to come out so you can move on to the next step, and finally to acceptance, where you can achieve closure."

"I suppose so." She looked up at him. Her voice almost pleaded for some type of enlightenment, some glimmer of comprehension about what had caused such a change in her father's lifestyle. "Even if there is a logical reason for his not telling me about his health, I still don't understand why he chose to live in such appalling conditions when he could certainly afford much better. And even if he couldn't afford it, he could have come to live with me. I would have willingly helped him. I…"

A sob caught in her throat and a single tear trickled down her cheek. The rest of her sentence came out as a barely audible whisper. "If only I'd known."

She swallowed and took a steadying breath, bringing

some control to her scattered emotions. "I shouldn't have said those things in front of Bobby." Intellectually she knew Shane was correct. Her anger was neither misplaced nor wrong, but that knowledge didn't negate her feelings of guilt about the spontaneous outburst. "He's too young to understand." Her voice dropped to a soft whisper, conveying her very real concerns. "I'm not even sure he really comprehends that his grandfather died."

Shane took a sip of his wine as he formulated his question. "Did Bobby know his grandfather very well?" He wasn't sure where it would take him. "Has Bobby always lived in Chicago?"

"Uh…yes." She, too, took another sip of her wine, to give herself time to collect her thoughts. "As I said, my father always came to my house for Christmas."

Shane gave a soft chuckle, partially forced, in an effort to appear casual in his conversation. "That seems a little backward. People usually take leave of the cold climates such as Chicago and spend the winter in places like southern Arizona or Florida."

"He visited us just two months ago. I was surprised when he called and said he was coming. He seemed fine then—" another sob caught in her throat "—but obviously he wasn't. He must have known his time was limited." She looked up at Shane, capturing his gaze and holding it. "I…I don't understand why he kept it from me."

Shane gave her hand a reassuring squeeze. "He probably didn't want to worry you. He thought you had enough to take care of without any added concerns."

She took a calming breath as she slowly withdrew her hand from the comfort of his touch. She wanted to change the subject, not so much because of his intimate gesture but rather her need to move away from the emotional circumstances of her father's death coupled with the entirely different pull of Shane's presence. "Well...you said you had something you wanted to talk to me about. What is it?"

He paused a moment as he adjusted to her change of topic. "Uh...yes. You said you'd be looking for a job as soon as you had your father's estate settled. I thought I might be able to help you. What kind of job are you looking for?"

Surprise crossed her face, almost as if she thought he must be kidding. "I'm an attorney, of course. If you recall, that's what I was going for when we—" She caught herself. She did not want to discuss the past with him, at least, not that specific event. "I've been practicing corporate law in Chicago ever since I finished law school."

He couldn't hide his surprise. "You're an attorney? I didn't know you'd completed your law degree." His voice softened almost to a whisper, as if he didn't want anyone to hear what he was saying. "When you disappeared—"

She cut off his words, a harsh edge clinging to her response. "I didn't *disappear*. You make it sound as if I just up and left one day for no reason." She quickly resumed what she'd been saying. She didn't want to give Shane a chance to bring up the past again. "I transferred to Phoenix and finished my classes there. I passed the Arizona bar exam, then was offered a position with a company in Chicago. I took the Illinois bar exam and moved to Chicago."

"Is that what you're going to look for here? You'd probably have better luck seeking out a corporate-attorney position in Tucson. It's only twenty-five miles away, and the commute is easy—it's a four-lane divided road."

"That's not really what I want to do. It's...well, it's part of why I wanted to move back to Pueblo." She shifted in the chair, seeking a more comfortable position as she warmed to the subject.

"I'd grown very dissatisfied with the corporate world—with the underhand dealings, the deception and the scramble to see how many people you can step on while clawing your way up the ladder to the top. I want to be able to apply my education and experience in a manner that will make a difference for the community. I have a son to raise, and I don't want him growing up believing that scrambling for power is what life's all about. I want to be able to show Bobby by example, rather than just telling him."

"Really?" Shane sat upright, showing a keen interest in what she was saying.

"I also wanted a safer place for Bobby, something away from the impersonal atmosphere of the big city but still close enough to a large urban area to be able to take advantage of the cultural and educational opportunities. As soon as we're settled in our own house, I'm going to take Bobby to Tucson to see the Desert Museum."

"It's a marvelous experience. He'll enjoy it." Shane ran his fingers lightly across her cheek. The tingle in his fingertips caused a quick intake of breath and made his heart beat a little faster.

"Everyone needs a day off occasionally to do something just for fun. The change of pace will be good for you, too. Maybe…" Was he about to get himself in deeper than he was ready to handle? "Maybe if I can free up my schedule, I could go with you." A little flicker of hope burned inside him. "We could make it an all-day outing—just the three of us."

Just the three of us. His words grabbed hold of Cynthia's senses and squeezed until she had to fight to keep from crying out in frustration. It was a very appealing picture, but one that could never be. No man had ever touched her soul and heated her desire the way Shane Fortune had—and still did. But facts were facts. She had been taken in before by his charm and persuasive manner and could not allow it to happen again. She could not risk what was best for her son on a momentary desire fueled by a past love. The stakes were too high.

Her gaze darted uneasily around the patio without resting on anything. What had begun to settle into a reasonably comfortable exchange had been jerked back into uncertainty and fear. She carefully chose her response, not wanting to show any adverse reaction to his words. "First I have to get everything settled, including finding a house for Bobby and me—" she chuckled nervously "—before we wear out our welcome here."

Shane leaned forward, resting his elbows on the table, and cupped her chin in his hand. "As I said earlier, you're more than welcome to stay as long as you need—or like."

The sensual warmth ran from the point where his fingers made contact with her skin across her face, then through her body. It was an intimate gesture that conveyed the type of closeness that had been missing from her life for the past six years. Her heart leapt and her pulse instantly shot up. A light-headedness came over her, almost a sensation of euphoria. She reveled briefly in the pleasure of the moment before forcing herself away from his seductive touch.

She knew it would take very little effort on his part to totally captivate her. It would be so easy for him. Her vulnerability pushed at her senses, telling her to get away. He placed his hand on top of hers, the movement so subtle and his touch so light that it took a second before she realized what he had done.

His soft voice carried a seductive quality that cut straight through her facade and settled over her desires. "It's interesting, your moving back to Pueblo with the desire to do something to give back to the community."

His words touched her, as well as filled her with anxiety.

The young man she'd fallen in love with back then had matured into a man of substance and integrity. Despite all her good intentions to steel herself against his magnetic pull, the magic of Shane Fortune had managed to work its way inside her—and it frightened her.

His voice created as much of a sensual feel as his fingers moving lightly across the back of her hand. All her instincts warned her that she was being lulled into a state of warm intimacy, yet she was helpless to prevent it. "I've tried to do that myself in various ways, too."

"Yes, so I've observed. Your children's hospital project is quite an impressive undertaking, and from what I've seen on the news, you're the driving force behind it."

"There are several of us involved in the hospital project, not just me. Since our family donated the land and Fortune Construction is building it, I seem to garner most of the press attention."

Cynthia's pulse raced, leaving her short of breath. The emotional pull of the moment was beginning to take its toll on her. She wanted to indulge the surprisingly comfortable feeling that had settled over her, a sensation of soft warmth combined with a tingle of excitement that only Shane Fortune could produce. She shook off the inappropriate desires. She didn't dare let down her guard.

Tactfully working her hand out of his grasp on the pretext of looking at her watch, she tried to sound casual yet matter-of-fact in her attitude—a far cry from the conflicting emotions churning inside her. "It's getting late and I've had an exhausting day. I think I'll turn in."

He reclaimed her hand. "It's not that late." He offered her an encouraging smile. "We haven't even finished our glass of wine. At least keep me company that much longer, okay?"

"I…" She knew what she *should* do, but she also knew

what she wanted to do. Her desires gained the upper hand. Her words might have been hesitant, but she said them, anyway. "Well, maybe for a little while."

They remained on the patio for another three hours talking about their careers and their plans for the future. She was willing to talk about her time in Chicago and her job as a corporate attorney, but she concentrated her conversation on what she wanted for the future. She avoided all but the vaguest generalities about Bobby. It was a time that had all the outward appearances of two people spending a comfortable evening getting reacquainted. But underneath ran a level of tension that kept each of them slightly on edge.

Cynthia tried to relax, but anxiety continued to drive her behavior. The warm familiarity of their conversation almost lulled her into a feeling of security and acceptance, but when Shane made a comment about Bobby, her panic leapt to the surface. She could no longer sit at the table as if nothing was wrong.

Rising from her chair, she pretended to stifle a yawn. "I really do need to get some sleep."

Shane collected the empty wineglasses and the bottle. "Let me get rid of these, and I'll walk upstairs with you." Something was wrong, but he couldn't figure out what. She kept vacillating between standoffish and amiable. One moment they were talking companionably and the next her guard was up. He carried everything to the kitchen, then hurried to catch up with her.

They silently climbed the stairs together. When they arrived at her bedroom, he grasped her hand before she could disappear behind a closed door. With his other hand he lightly touched her cheek, then tucked an errant lock of hair behind her ear.

"Thank you for sharing a glass of wine with me. I enjoyed the opportunity to spend this time with you."

His voice and words once again settled over her like a soft caress. Cynthia's anxiety level increased in direct proportion to her quickening heartbeat, leaving her confused and unsettled. "Thank you."

He leaned in close to her as he continued to clasp her hand. In fact, he was too close. She wanted to move away, but her back was already against the doorjamb. Then came the precise moment she both desired and feared—he lowered his mouth to hers. He brushed her lips with his as if testing to see what she would allow, then pulled her into an embrace. A moment later his mouth fully covered hers.

She hesitated. The best thing for her to do was pull away from him. She needed to put a stop to what was happening before it got totally out of control. That's what she *should* do, but it was not where her desires led her. Her determination and her resolve melted away, draining her of any hope that she might be able to resist his advances. She ignored everything except the pull of his magnetism while slipping her arms around his neck.

All the heat, all the fire and all the passion that had ever existed between them exploded in an incendiary flash. She had missed him even more than she'd allowed herself to believe—his touch, his embrace and the ecstasy of his kiss. She fought her feelings, however, for she desperately needed to bring some sort of sense and logic to what was happening. Full-blown panic set in, enabling her to finally break off the kiss. Her words were half breathless delight and half mounting fear. "No…don't…"

A very shaken Cynthia hurried into her bedroom and closed the door. She leaned back against it and tried to gulp in a calming breath. It did nothing to soothe the excitement coursing through her veins or alleviate her fears about what had just happened. She touched her trembling fingers to her lips. She could still feel the burning passion that conveyed the essence of Shane Fortune, an ardor that infused her with a hunger mere food could never satisfy.

A soft knock on the door jarred her out of her thoughts, followed by the sound of Shane calling her name. She didn't dare answer. She knew she did not possess the emotional strength to resist his advances a second time, regardless of how sincere her intentions. A sigh of relief escaped her lips when she heard him walk down the hall.

Shane went directly to his bedroom. He'd felt the fire and tasted the earthiness of her kiss when she'd slipped her arms around his neck. There was no doubt that the old spark still existed between them. But as quickly as it had ignited he found himself staring at a closed door. If she had been someone new in his life, he would be better equipped to deal with it, to know what to say and what to do. But that wasn't the case. They shared an intense history, and he'd ended up hurting her badly, something that had come back to haunt him now more than ever.

Five

Cynthia stared at herself in the bathroom mirror, not at all happy with the reflection that stared back. She had spent a miserable night torn between two extremes. On one side was the heated desire Shane's kiss had sparked and the memories of a love that she had thought would last forever. On the other side was a very unsettling confusion that enveloped her in layers of guilt and anxiety.

Every word she spoke, everything she did, indeed, the very core of her thoughts, all culminated in Shane Fortune and their unexpected involvement after all these years. She had everything under control, had carefully established the parameters of a *keep your distance* situation—until last night.

When she let him kiss her and, worse yet, returned that kiss, she betrayed everything she'd fought so hard to establish. She had allowed Shane Fortune back into her life on an emotional level. He had to be made to understand it was only one isolated incident. It did not open the door to anything more, not now and not ever.

Bobby was her priority. She had to figure out what was best for her son. Shane had offered no apologies for the past, not even an explanation. All his good work for the community did not erase that fact. He seemed to want to renew their physical relationship, but had shown no interest in repairing their emotional one. As much as Shane's touch excited every corner of her existence, she could not subject Bobby to the same type of seemingly arbitrary treatment as she had experienced.

As much as she wanted to stay in her bedroom until after Shane left for work, she needed to get downstairs quickly. She didn't dare take a chance on a repeat of the other morning when Bobby and Shane had had all that time together—time in which Shane could question the boy about his father. She had to make sure Shane understood that last night's kiss would never lead anywhere. It was a mistake, nothing more. A veil of sorrow descended over her. If only she really believed that herself.

She forced a calm to the inner turmoil that continued to plague her, then went downstairs to face what the day had to offer.

"Good morning." Shane extended a pleasant smile when she entered the kitchen, but his eyes sent a different message. They conveyed uneasiness, and seemed to be searching inside her. A shiver darted across the back of her neck. She wasn't sure what he was searching for, but it made her uncomfortable.

She forced an outer show of confidence. "Good morning." She glanced around the kitchen. "Is Bobby here?"

"I haven't seen him. I assumed he was still sleeping." Shane reached for the coffeepot. "May I pour you a cup?"

She didn't answer. "Before he comes downstairs…"

she said, then took a deep breath and slowly exhaled. But the anxiety refused to go away. It jittered through her body at an alarming rate. "There's something we need to get straight. About last night…the, uh…" She nervously cleared her throat as she shifted her weight from one foot to the other. "Well, it never should have happened."

He set the coffeepot on the counter and gave her a questioning look. "The kiss? And just why do you think it shouldn't have happened?"

He looked so desirable, so damned sexy. A tingling sensation reverberated through her body. To calm her racing pulse and pounding heart, she had to avert her gaze. "We've traveled that road before, and for whatever reason—" a moment of despair jabbed her as the painful memory filtered through the wall of her determination "—it didn't work out. There's no use repeating history." She turned away from him as she glanced toward the stairs. "I have business to take care of and a son to raise. I don't need any more complications in my life than I already have."

"That's what I represent to you?" He filled a mug with coffee and set it on the counter in front of her. "A complication?"

The butterflies played havoc with her stomach and sent her emotions into overdrive. All it took was one look from him, a raised eyebrow and the tilt of his head. His gaze cut right through her defenses and struck directly at her vulnerability.

She refused to answer his question. Even if she wanted to, she didn't know how to respond to it. "I have a very busy day ahead of me, so I'd better get Bobby up and dressed." She took the coffee mug and hurried out of the kitchen, thankful to be away from his scrutiny and unsettling questions and the devastating pull of his sexuality.

Shane watched her go. For someone who'd spent his entire life displaying an outwardly decisive attitude, he couldn't find any comfortable ground when talking to Cynthia—at least not comfortable as he chose to define it, where he at least had control of his emotions, if not the circumstances. She was more beautiful than ever and definitely more desirable than ever, but she had changed. There were many levels to her that he had never known before, more depth than he remembered. Had these things always been there and he had been so absorbed in his own search for identity that he hadn't noticed? If that was true, then he'd screwed up even worse than he thought.

He'd felt her heated response to his kiss, however brief, before she pulled away from him. In his heart and soul he *knew* that she still felt something for him. He tasted it in her kiss and sensed it in the very air around them. But what to do about it? How to get past that wall she'd built between them?

He slumped back against the counter, making no effort to suppress a sigh of despair. It was a wall he'd helped her build, and no matter how much he tried to convince himself otherwise, he couldn't escape the truth. He had supplied the mortar that held the bricks together when he'd abruptly terminated their affair and dismissed her from his life. It had been his decision, and now he was suffering the consequences of his behavior. It was up to him to find a way to fix it. The first thing he needed to do was make sure he kept the lines of communication open.

He turned his hand to making breakfast for the three of them. He paused a moment as those exact words hit him— the *three* of them. A warm sensation spread through his body, something he wanted to explore. A little frown wrinkled across his forehead as another thought seeped into his mind. He still didn't know why Cynthia had been left to raise her son alone. He wanted to know what had happened, but didn't know how to go about asking without seeming to be prying into her private business, something she'd made very clear she would not tolerate. He turned the problem over in his mind as he poured three glasses of orange juice and set them on the table.

A moment later Bobby came bounding into the kitchen full of enthusiasm, still dressed in his pajamas.

"Good morning, champ. You ready for breakfast, or do you want to get dressed first?"

Bobby climbed onto the chair. "I'm hungry." He reached for his glass of orange juice.

"Hold on there. Don't you think we should wait for your mother to join us?"

"She'll be here in a little bit. She said she has to pull herself together first."

"Pull herself together?" A quick hit of panic stopped Shane in his tracks. "Is she okay?"

"I guess so."

"Bobby!" Cynthia rushed through the door, flustered by what she'd heard. Her momentary eye contact with Shane sent a flush of embarrassment across her cheeks.

She slowed her words and movements so Bobby wouldn't think he'd done something wrong. She gave him a loving smile. "Don't you think you'd better get dressed before you have breakfast?"

He looked up at his mother. "But I'm hungry, and Shane already fixed breakfast, so I need to eat it right away." He turned his attention to Shane. "Isn't that right, Shane?"

Cynthia shot Shane the same look she had earlier, the one that said Bobby was her son and she didn't want any interference. He gave Bobby's hair a friendly tousle. "I can't help you there, champ." He leaned down to whisper in Bobby's ear, making sure it was loud enough for Cynthia to hear. "I'll guard your breakfast until you get back."

An unhappy Bobby stomped up the stairs toward his bedroom.

"Well, are you together yet?" Shane asked Cynthia. There was no mistaking the amusement in his voice. He blatantly looked her up and down as he walked around her. "Exactly where is it that you came apart?"

His close scrutiny of her physical being sent a tingle of excitement dancing across her skin. She picked up the coffeepot and refilled her mug. She tried to sound nonchalant, as if the words Bobby had heard her say had no meaning and the way Shane was looking at her didn't have any affect on her senses. "You know children. They hear something and don't understand what you really mean."

"Oh? What did you really mean?"

She took a sip of her coffee before responding. "I simply meant that I wanted to run a brush through my hair first." Her gaze darted nervously around the room.

"I see." He reached out and touched her hair, then traced her jaw before breaking off the physical contact. The tactile pleasure lingered on his fingertips even after he withdrew his hand. "You look very nice. But then, you looked nice a few minutes ago when you came downstairs the first time."

He didn't believe her explanation, but realized that pursuing it would not be the best course of action. "So, tell me...what's on your agenda for today? Are you making any headway with your father's estate?"

Her frustration with the problem spoke as loudly as her words. "Some, but it's going slower than I'd anticipated. I still can't believe what a mess it is. Fortunately I've been able so far to avoid spending long hours standing in lines at various government offices here and at the county seat in Tucson. I think I'm going to have to take at least half a day to handle some of the details in Tucson and another day to drive up to Phoenix to deal with the state offices. Doing that in person will be quicker and easier in the long run.''

Shane perked up at this bit of information. ''When will you be going to Phoenix? I have some business to take care of in Phoenix, too.'' He touched his fingertips to her cheek. Regardless of his intentions, he couldn't stop himself from touching her. The feel of her silky skin sent a ripple of excitement through his body. He cupped her chin in his hand and lifted her face so he could look into her eyes. ''I have a real busy schedule for the next couple of days, but after that...'' His voice was as tentative as his question. ''Perhaps we could drive up together?''

Cynthia stepped away from the unnerving sensation of his touch and the decidedly sensual pull it exerted on her. She ran her hand across her nape to still the tremor caused by the physical contact. A shiver made its way through her body. His dark eyes seemed to be looking directly into her soul as if searching for something. She suddenly felt very tired, as if something had drained off all her energy. ''I...I don't know. I may not have to go at all.''

Bobby ran into the kitchen and quickly secured his place at the table. A grateful Cynthia took advantage of the interruption to break the spell Shane's presence had begun to weave around her. With each physical encounter, it became more difficult for her to turn away.

The next couple of days were very busy for Cynthia. She had things narrowed down to the point where she could not proceed any further without going to Phoenix and also spending several hours in Tucson. But that presented her with the problem of what to do about Bobby. It was unfair to expect a five-year-old boy to spend long hours waiting in lines to deal with bureaucrats and various government agencies.

That evening a tired Cynthia put Bobby to bed, then took a glass of iced tea out onto the patio. She allowed her mind to wander. She had barely seen Shane in the past couple of days. He'd left the house early and gotten home late. That had given her a break from trying to juggle the emotional pull he exerted on her while she dealt with the stressful situation of putting her father's estate in order.

She took a sip from her glass, then placed it on the table. She leaned back in her chair. The fatigue spread through her entire body. Her legs and arms felt as heavy as lead. At the moment she wasn't sure she could even move them. Her shoulder muscles had knotted into an uncomfortable tightness.

A jolt of adrenaline shot through her body. She stiffened to a startled attention as two hands began to massage the tension out of her shoulders. She twisted around in her chair and saw Shane. Relief settled over her as a weary smile tugged at the corners of her mouth. "You startled me." She settled back into her chair. "I didn't realize you were home. How long have you been here?"

"I just arrived." He continued to massage her shoulders. "I was headed toward the stairs when I saw you out here." He glanced around the patio. "Is Bobby already in bed?"

"Yes. It was his bedtime fifteen minutes ago."

"I guess I didn't realize it was that late." His dexterous fingers worked with tender efficiency to ease the tightness from her muscles. "You look tired. Have you had a tough day? Your shoulders are tied in knots."

"Mmm...that feels good." A little moan of pleasure

escaped her throat. "It's been more frustrating and emotionally exhausting than physically tiring, but I can tell it's beginning to take its toll on me."

"Are you getting close to wrapping everything up?"

"I'm at the point where I need to go to Phoenix for the day to visit some state-government offices. I thought I could handle things by phone and fax, but it's not working out that way. What I need to do first is make some sort of arrangement for Bobby." She paused for a moment, then turned toward him. "Do you know of a good day-care center that could take Bobby for a day or two? Perhaps someone at the hospital who could give me a recommendation?"

He stopped massaging her shoulders and sat down next to her at the table. "There are several good ones, but I have a better idea. My sister. Isabelle."

"What about her?"

"She's engaged to Brad Rowan and right now is in the middle of planning her wedding. She can make those plans from my house as easily as anywhere else. She can keep an eye on Bobby. That way, he won't have to be disrupted. He can stay here where he's comfortable and familiar with the surroundings. He'll have his own toys and the swimming pool."

His suggestion caught her by surprise. "Oh, no—I couldn't do that. There's no way I could impose on Isabelle. If you could just give me the name of a couple of good day-care centers, I'll call them first thing in the morning."

"Nonsense. You know Bobby will be more comfortable here. I'd take care of him myself, but I'm not able to clear my schedule and cancel my appointments this week. I'm going to call Isabelle right now. When do you want to go to Phoenix?"

"I'd like to go as soon as possible. I was hoping that tomorrow I'd be able to find a place for Bobby so I could drive up to Phoenix the next day and then Tucson the day after that."

"I'll be right back."

Shane went to the kitchen to make the phone call. He dialed Isabelle's number, and after two rings she answered the phone.

"Isabelle, it's Shane. I could use your help with something."

"What is it?"

"I don't know whether you've heard—" An amusing thought interrupted what he was going to say. "Kate may be avoiding me, but I'm sure you've spoken to her in the last few days. Anyway, as I'm sure you know, Cynthia McCree has returned to Pueblo. She and her son…" Once again thoughts about the identity of Bobby's father and where he was now popped into his mind leaving him with an uneasy feeling. He filed the thoughts away, saving the speculation for another time. "—have been staying with me until she can get her father's estate settled and find a place of her own."

"Yes, Kate did mention something about it."

"Cynthia needs to go to Phoenix tomorrow and then to Tucson the following day on business. She was asking me about a day-care center for Bobby, but she's only going to be gone a little while. So…"

Isabelle's laugh traveled across the phone line. "…so, you want to know if I'll watch her son while she's gone."

"Well…yes, that's it. Bobby is familiar with the surroundings, his toys are here, and he loves the swimming pool. There's no reason to disrupt his routine by sending him off to some strange place for only a couple of days. You're working on your wedding plans. You could do that here as easily as there. So, what do you say? Can you come over tomorrow morning and spend the day with Bobby?''

''I think so. Brad's here right now. Let me check with him to make sure he doesn't have something else planned for us. Hold on.''

Shane bristled at the mention of Brad's name. The man would soon be his brother-in-law, and as such he would have to maintain at least a civil attitude around him. He heard Brad and Isabelle talking, but he couldn't make out what they were saying. A minute later Isabelle returned to the phone.

''No problem. I'll see you first thing in the morning.''

Shane talked to Isabelle for a couple of minutes longer, then returned to the patio. Cynthia had her head back and her eyes closed. He brushed his fingertips lightly across her cheek, taking pleasure in the silky smooth texture. He felt a rush of exhilaration, just as he experienced every time he came in physical contact with her.

His mind flooded with memories of the many nights they had spent making passionate love, of what he had come later to recognize as being as much emotional as physical. An undeniable desire to take care of her invaded his thoughts, a desire to banish the weariness he saw in her face. It was a familiar place for him, but from what he had observed of this *new* Cynthia, she was not one to sit back and allow someone else to take charge of her life.

He shook away the errant thoughts and comforting possibilities and replaced them with reality. Regardless of the newly discovered similarities in their life goals, he still wasn't sure how Cynthia McCree would fit into the demands of his lifestyle and plans.

He once again found himself trying to straddle two worlds. This time, however, his commitment to his dual ancestry was on one side and Cynthia McCree was on the other. He brushed his fingertips across her cheek again and touched her hair. The excitement flowed through his veins and heated his desire. And his confusion and uncertainty increased in equal measure. He didn't seem to be able to keep away from the physical contact with her, however fleeting. He *needed* to know she was really there and not just a figment of his imagination. And he wanted so much more.

He smiled as he spoke, hoping it would cover his troubled thoughts. "Isabelle said she'd stay with Bobby, so you can take care of your business. She'll be here first thing in the morning."

Cynthia shifted her position in the chair in an attempt to subtly move away from the warmth of his touch, even though she found it both comforting and stimulating. She was accustomed to making her own decisions and taking care of her problems without any help, but she had to admit it was nice to have someone else see to her well-being, if only for a brief time.

"That's very kind of Isabelle. It'll sure be a big help to me. I hope it's not too much of an inconvenience for her."

"Not at all. She's looking forward to seeing you again."

Cynthia stifled a yawn as she looked at her watch. "It's getting late." A hint of anxiety tickled at the edges of her consciousness. Things were beginning to feel too comfortable, too much like a family relationship. It was something she could not allow to happen. There was no way she could take a chance on jeopardizing her son's security by subjecting him to the uncertainty of Shane's reaction to learning he was Bobby's father. "I'd better get my paperwork organized tonight so I don't end up wasting time in the morning." She stood up, retrieved her empty iced-tea glass from the table and carried it into the kitchen.

Shane followed her. As soon as she deposited the glass on the kitchen counter, he pulled her into his arms. He felt her body stiffen, then soften. He didn't know if it was because she was tired or if she'd managed to set aside some of her initial wariness, but whatever the reason, he detected the change. He knew he wanted her. He didn't even try to kid himself about that. But under what circumstances? That question was not as easily answered.

He banished the disturbing thoughts from his mind by lowering his head and capturing her mouth with his. It started as a gentle kiss. The warmth and caring that had always been a part of her instantly infused him with the earthy passion that had once been his life. He tightened his embrace and deepened the kiss. He felt her hesitation, then her arms circled his neck. He had intended for it to be a kiss and nothing more. Nothing, that was, until he felt the heat of her response. Then the fire that had been burning inside him all day exploded into reality.

He slipped his tongue between her lips. Her intoxicating taste instantly filled his mouth. His heart pounded with a primal desire that he desperately wanted to satisfy. No woman had ever elicited such a strong and immediate response from him the way she did—the way she always had, ever since their first meeting. He twined his fingers in her hair and reaffirmed his control of her mouth. His tongue explored, his lips teased, his ardor deepened.

The surprising depth of her response drove him wild. His body told him one thing—to sweep her up in his arms, carry her to his bedroom and spend the rest of the night making love to her. But the tenuous thread of sense and logic that still clung to his consciousness told him to be cautious.

His ardor increased as he shoved the wayward thought from his mind. Sense and logic be damned. Nobody ignited his passions the way Cynthia McCree did, and no one ever would. He wanted her back in his life—not for just a night, not for just a couple of weeks. He wanted her—body and soul—forever.

He twined his fingers in her long blond tresses and pulled her close. He felt her breasts press against his chest with every breath she drew. The heat settled low in his body.

Full-blown panic raced through Cynthia. How easy it had been for him. A touch, a caress, and she was once again putty in his hands. She broke away and fought to bring her ragged breathing under control. She couldn't remember the last time she'd been as frightened. Her words came out as a breathless whisper. "Don't. I..." She couldn't force out any more words. She saw the confusion and uncertainty in his eyes. She turned and ran toward the stairs and the safety of her bedroom.

Isabelle Fortune grabbed her purse from the table and followed Brad Rowan out the front door and into the car.

Brad put the car in gear and backed out of the driveway. His brow furrowed in concentration. "Hmm."

"What's the matter, Brad?"

"Have you ever met this Cynthia McCree? It seems to me a bit presumptuous of Shane to ask this favor of you."

"Cynthia and Shane dated several years ago, before she moved away. I met her a couple of times, but don't know her that well."

"You're sure this isn't too early in the morning to be arriving at Shane's house?"

Isabelle glanced at her watch. "He said Cynthia wanted to get an early start to Phoenix, and I should be there no later than seven-thirty. We're right on time. It's nice of you to pick me up and drive me over there, especially at this hour. I know how busy you are.''

He smiled at her and reached over to give her hand a squeeze. ''It's my pleasure. Besides, I have something I want to talk to Shane about, and this might be a good time to catch him away from his office at the hospital.''

Soon Brad pulled the car into Shane's driveway. A moment later Shane admitted them to the house. He gave Isabelle a warm hug, but the handshake he gave Brad was more perfunctory than personal. He ushered them into the kitchen.

''Isabelle, you remember Cynthia.''

''Of course.'' Isabelle smiled graciously. ''It's so nice to see you again. Shane tells me you've moved back to Pueblo.''

Shane continued his introductions. ''And this is Bobby.'' He turned his attention to the little boy. ''This is my sister, Isabelle. She's going to keep you company today.''

Bobby stared at Isabelle for a moment, then grinned. ''Hi.''

Shane introduced Brad to Cynthia and Bobby. Isabelle poured herself a cup of coffee and joined Bobby and Cynthia. They quickly became engaged in conversation.

Brad edged toward the kitchen door. ''I'd like a word with you, Shane, if you have a minute.''

Shane was not pleased with this turn of events. ''All right. Let's go into the den.''

The two men did so, and Shane closed the door behind them they could talk in private. He turned to face Brad. ''So, what's on your mind?''

''I'm a little worried about all the publicity surrounding your comments concerning Lightfoot Plateau.''

Shane eyed him warily. "And just what is it that bothers you?"

Brad chuckled nervously. "You make it sound like I'm doing something bad just because I won't sell you the land. I have every intention of giving it to Isabelle as a wedding present—after we're married."

Shane set his jaw in a hard determined line, making no effort to hide his dislike for Brad Rowan. "I want that land outright, a nice clean sale with no strings attached and no promises of what you're going to do *someday*."

Brad's voice took on a matter-of-fact tone. "It's like I told you—it will be a wedding present to Isabelle—*after* we're married. That's the best I can do."

"That's not good enough." Shane paused a moment to take in Brad's nervousness. He carefully measured his words. "I *will* get possession of that land. You will *never* be able to develop it, because the Fortunes have the where-withal to stop your plans, or at the very least delay them for so long they're no longer viable."

Shane started for the door, signaling that their conversation was over. Then he turned back to Brad and fixed him with a cold stare. He dropped his voice to a low timbre, leaving no question about his intent. "And that's a promise."

Shane quickly composed himself as he left Brad in the den and returned to Cynthia and Isabelle. He smiled warmly as if to say nothing was wrong. "Have you two ladies worked everything out?"

"We sure have," Isabelle replied. "Bobby and I are going to spend this afternoon together while Cynthia goes to Tucson, and then we'll spend the entire day together tomorrow while she's in Phoenix." She turned to Bobby. "Isn't that right?"

"Yeah! We're gonna go swimming."

Shane's brow furrowed in confusion. He looked at Cynthia. "I thought you were going to Phoenix today."

"This afternoon, then all day tomorrow works out better for Isabelle's schedule. She's going to leave now, but she'll come back after lunch and I'll drive to Tucson."

"I guess there's nothing more I can do here, so if you ladies will excuse me, I need to get to the hospital." Shane took a final drink from his coffee cup and set it in the sink. He reached over and tousled Bobby's hair. "I'll see you tonight, champ."

As Shane turned toward the door leading to the garage, he caught sight of Brad entering the kitchen. He shot the man one last hard glance, then continued out to his car. He had more-immediate things on his mind.

He wanted to spend some time with Bobby when Cynthia wasn't around to intervene. He could tell from her protective attitude around her son that she'd never consent to leaving Bobby with him, although he didn't know why. It was the reason he had drawn Isabelle into it. His curiosity about the boy increased every time he saw Bobby, filling him with questions about who Bobby's father was and where the man was now. And still the one nagging thought about Bobby's possible parentage—the concept that continued to lurk in the back of his mind without crystallizing into a clear thought—had a very unsettling effect on him and he didn't know why.

Six

Cynthia glanced at the clock. Isabelle would be arriving any minute. She cleared away the lunch dishes as Bobby drained the last drop of milk from his glass.

"Can I go swimming now, Mommy?"

"Not right away. You know you have to rest first." She had long ago given up trying to get the rambunctious little boy to take a nap, but she still tried to get him to spend some quiet time with a book. "If you stay quiet for an hour, you can go swimming."

She turned toward the sound of the front door opening. "That must be Isabelle now." She called out, "We're in the kitchen." But it was Shane who made an appearance a moment later.

"Am I in time for lunch?"

"I thought you were Isabelle." She eyed him suspiciously, not sure what to make of his unexpected arrival. "What are you doing here? Yesterday you said you had a very busy schedule."

"Yesterday I did have a busy schedule. Today, however, is another matter." He glanced at the dirty dishes stacked on the counter. "Well, it looks like you've already eaten. Do you have enough left for another person?"

"I suppose so." An edge of irritation crept into her voice. "So what happened to your usually busy schedule?"

"Today's lunch meeting turned into a breakfast meeting for tomorrow morning. So I thought I'd come home for lunch, see if there was anything Isabelle needed."

"I see. Then you'll be returning to work after lunch?"

He cocked his head and stared at her for a moment, a hint of puzzlement crossing his face. "Yes. I have patients to see. Is there a problem?"

"No. Of course not. I was just surprised to see you, that's all." Her first thought was born of panic. Had Shane shown up thinking she was already on her way to Tucson? Was it an attempt to get close to Bobby? Her anxiety level increased dramatically. Did he suspect the truth? She reined in her runaway thoughts. She could not allow her fears to jump out of control at each and every little incident. She had to keep the situation in its proper perspective. There certainly wasn't anything wrong with his deciding to have lunch at home when his business plans changed.

"Hi." Isabelle's voice floated in from the entry hall. "I'm here." A moment later she appeared at the kitchen door.

"Shane—I was surprised to see your car in the driveway. What are you doing here?"

An amused chuckle escaped this throat. "That's the same thing Cynthia asked me. If I didn't know better, I'd think I wasn't welcome in my own home." He shot a look at Cynthia as if to ask if there was some truth to that.

* * *

A few hours later Cynthia drove through the entrance of the Saguaro Springs gated community and down the street toward Shane's house. As soon as she pulled up to the curb, she realized Isabelle's car wasn't in the driveway. Had she and Bobby gone somewhere? An uncomfortable sensation pricked at her consciousness. She found the front door unlocked. Her uneasiness jumped to apprehension. She stepped into the entrance foyer. Sounds of laughter came from the backyard.

She hurried through the den, coming to an abrupt halt in front of the sliding glass doors. A hard jolt of panic grabbed her. Isabelle was nowhere in sight. Bobby was splashing around in the shallow end of the pool—with Shane.

It was a scene that would have warmed anyone's heart— a father and son laughing and playing together—but it left Cynthia unnerved and scared. She tried to swallow her panic, but to no avail. She stepped out onto the patio.

Bobby's face lit up when he saw her. ''Mommy! Watch what Shane taught me.''

Before she could say anything, Bobby ducked beneath the surface, put his arms in front of him and started kicking his feet. He swam underwater to the side of the pool, then popped up. A big grin spread across his face. ''Did you see me?''

She forced a smile as she walked across the patio toward the pool. ''I sure did. You looked great.''

''Shane taught me how to swim underwater. Isn't that neat?'' He scrambled up the steps, then ran around the edge of the pool. ''Here I come—bombs away!'' He jumped into the water.

She glared down at Shane in the water, as much annoyed by his expression of innocence as she was frightened about what he and Bobby might have talked about. Shane had obviously been here for a while. Could he have been with Bobby all afternoon, sending Isabelle home as soon as she'd left for Tucson?

She couldn't keep the irritation out of her voice. "What are you doing here?"

Shane put his hands on the decking and pushed himself out of the pool. He sat on the edge with his legs dangling in the water. He looked at her, still the picture of innocence. "That's the second time you've asked me that today. I do live here, you know."

She swung her gaze to Bobby as he climbed out of the pool. She clenched her jaw and lowered her voice so Bobby wouldn't hear her. "You know very well what I mean. Your busy day, your need to return to the hospital to see patients following lunch."

"Oh, yeah, that." Shane grinned at her, his features taking on the look of someone who'd just pulled off what he thought was the perfect prank, then ended up getting caught.

"Yeah, *that.*" She fought to keep her expression stern, to make her displeasure with him obvious, but it became more difficult with each passing second. The late-afternoon sun glinted off the water droplets in his raven hair and enhanced the golden hue of his tan. His broad shoulders and chest had not lost any of their muscle tone over the years, nor had his long legs. He was still the sexiest and most desirable man she had ever seen. She tried to steel herself against the powerful pull, as much emotional as physical.

"Well—" he stood up and grabbed two towels from the chair, handing one to Bobby, who'd arrived on the scene with curiosity etched across his features "—it seems that my afternoon caseload wasn't as heavy as I'd thought. It only took me an hour or so to finish up, so I came back here and let Isabelle go home. Bobby and I spent the afternoon in the pool.''

He grinned at Bobby. ''I wouldn't swear to it, but I think he must be part fish the way he loves the water.''

''Yes, he's always loved the water. That's one of the top things I'm looking for in a house—a swimming pool.'' The tension spread through her body. She took the towel from Bobby and stooped to dry his back.

Shane and Bobby had spent most of the afternoon together. Bobby didn't seem upset by anything. In fact, it was blatantly obvious how much the two of them had enjoyed the afternoon. The other thing that was equally obvious was the fact that Shane was doing everything he could to get close to Bobby. What was not as obvious was why. Did he suspect the truth?

Shane looped his towel around his neck, hanging on to the ends with his hands. ''Why don't you put on your swimsuit and come into the water with us?''

Bobby squirmed out of her reach. He stood next to Shane, looping his towel around his neck and holding the ends in the exact same way as Shane. ''Yeah, Mommy. Come swimming with us.''

She smoothed back Bobby's wet hair. Her son's actions in mimicking his father and the bond that seemed to be forming between them stabbed at her. Waves of guilt swept through her, settling in the pit of her stomach in a sickening swirl. She managed to force what she hoped was an outer calm to her manner. A little shiver moved across the surface of her skin. Her life of late revolved around trying to maintain a facade to hide her true feelings. ''Don't you think you've had enough for one day? It's almost dinnertime.''

''Shane said he'd order pizza for us when you got home. We can play in the water until it comes.'' The little boy looked up at her, his eyes pleading. "Can we, Mommy? Huh? Can we?"

"Yes, Mommy…can we?" Shane's eyes sparkled with mischief as he echoed Bobby's entreaty. He reached out to take her hand, but she quickly moved out of his reach. His mischievous look changed to a questioning one.

"Maybe some other time." She saw the disappointment on her son's face, and it tore her up inside. She swallowed the lump in her throat and quickly blinked away the tears starting to form in her eyes. He was such a good boy and asked for so little, but there was no way that participating in a *family* playtime in the swimming pool could be for anyone's benefit. "Go up to your room and get dressed, and I'll start dinner."

"Aw, gee." Bobby stomped off toward the den with a scowl on his face, his displeasure known to one and all.

As soon as Bobby was out of sight, she turned to Shane, making no attempt to hide her irritation. She snapped out her anger. "I'll thank you not to interfere with my instructions to my son. He's *my* responsibility, not yours."

She regretted the words the moment she said them. She started to apologize, but before she could say anything, Shane cocked his head and shot her a questioning look. Was that skepticism she saw in his eyes?

"I…I'm sorry," she said. "I didn't mean for that to sound so harsh. It's just that sometimes it's difficult raising a child by yourself and…" She didn't know how to finish.

Shane gently brushed his fingertips across her cheek, then tucked a stray lock of hair behind her ear. She bristled at the intimate gesture. He'd caught her at a vulnerable moment, but that didn't mean she needed to let him take advantage of it.

"Stop that. If I wanted my hair there, I would have put

it there." She ran her fingers through her hair to bring the stray lock forward again.

He seemed unfazed by her actions. "You've done a terrific job with Bobby. He's a great kid." He touched her cheek again. The physical contact sent a renewed surge of excitement through her body. She quickly stepped away from the heated temptation before it could totally overwhelm her.

"Yes, he is." She dropped her voice to a near whisper as the emotion cloaked her words. "He's the most important thing in my life. I don't know what I'd do if I ever lost him."

Shane furrowed his brow in confusion. "Lost him? What do you mean by that?" He hesitated a moment before venturing his next question. His words were filled with genuine concern. "Is there some problem?"

"No. Of course not. I only meant that if something happened to him…if he should be in an accident or become seriously ill or…"

Cynthia's words trailed off. After seeing Shane and Bobby in the pool, seeing the bond forming between them and the way Bobby idolized Shane, a whole new fear had reached out and grabbed her—one that scared her more than the possibility of Shane's rejection. The tears started to form in her eyes again as a horrible trepidation tried to take hold. What if Shane instituted a custody suit and tried to take Bobby away from her? She quickly turned her head so Shane wouldn't see her pain and her fear. She hurried toward the door, leaving him standing by the pool.

Shane watched as she disappeared into the house. A mass of conflicting thoughts whirled through his head. There was no question in his mind that some sort of problem existed, but what? If Bobby was ill, it certainly didn't show. In his professional medical opinion, the boy was strong and healthy.

Could it be that there was some sort of custody suit between Cynthia and Bobby's father? He had tried to subtly introduce the topic of Bobby's father during the course of the afternoon, but all he got in return was a vague response from Bobby about his father *going away* before he was born. The statement left him uneasy, even though he didn't know exactly how to interpret it.

And still, the nagging thought in the back of his mind kept poking at his consciousness, the one trying to tell him Bobby was more than just *Cynthia's* son.

Shane towel-dried his hair as he crossed the patio toward the house. He went straight to his bedroom and dressed in a pair of old jeans and a T-shirt. When he emerged from his bedroom, he spotted Bobby at the top of the stairs and caught up to him.

"Sorry about the pizza, champ. Maybe we can do that another night."

"Can we?" Bobby's face brightened at the prospect.

"You bet we can." Shane started down the stairs with Bobby beside him. "Do you like to play ball? I have an old baseball. Would you like to go out in the yard and play catch until dinner is ready?"

"Yeah!" A big grin spread across the boy's face as he raced down the stairs ahead of Shane.

After a quick detour through the utility room to get the ball out of a storage closet, Shane joined Bobby in the yard. "You ready? Here it comes." Not sure of the little boy's skills, he tossed the ball gently. Bobby caught it at first, then dropped it. He quickly scooped it up and threw it back to Shane, who had to stretch to get the wild throw before it hit the side of the house.

* * *

Cynthia watched them from the kitchen window—a father and son playing ball in the yard, laughing and having fun. What could be more perfect? A sharp pang of guilt shot through her, followed closely by a deep sorrow that brought tears to her eyes again. An important factor missing from Bobby's life—something that had been a concern for Cynthia—was someone for him to do *guy* stuff with, an adult male presence who could teach him things she couldn't. She had been both mother and father to Bobby, but she could only do so much. There were times when a boy needed a man.

She finished making dinner, then called to Bobby to wash his hands and come to the table. A moment later Shane stepped into the kitchen and held out his hands. A teasing grin played around the corners of his mouth.

"My hands are clean. Is it okay if I have dinner, too?"

Cynthia shot him a withering look. Her words were laced with sarcasm. "Cute. Real cute."

Bobby ran into the kitchen and took his place at the table. He stared at the food in front of him. "Shane says we can still have pizza, just not tonight."

She glanced at Shane but was surprised to find him paying attention to Bobby, rather than taunting her with this latest attempt to win Bobby over...*if* that was what he was doing.

Dinner turned into a disturbing time for Cynthia. Shane appeared to be enjoying himself, and she could see the excitement bubbling out of her son. Once again she presented an upbeat facade, but inside was an entirely different story. It tore at her heart and played to her worst fear to see Bobby becoming so attached to Shane. And she had to admit that Shane seemed genuinely fond of Bobby, too. Did she dare to hope that he would be able to accept her son—*their* son—without trying to take him away?

Following dinner, she wanted to spend some time with Bobby, quality time, where they would share the events of the day and usually read a book together. Even though he would not be starting first grade until the fall, he could already read from the second-grade reading books and had mastered the basics of simple arithmetic. But all Bobby wanted to talk about was how much fun he'd had with Shane, how Shane taught him to swim underwater, how Shane played catch with him. It was not the type of quality time Cynthia had hoped for.

After finally getting Bobby to bed, she wandered out to the patio to enjoy the pleasant night air. Sitting at the table, Cynthia turned everything over in her mind. She had not been this confused and uncertain about things since Shane had terminated their relationship two weeks before she'd discovered she was pregnant. She stared at the shimmering water of the pool without really seeing it as the emotional tidal wave washed over her. A sob caught in her throat and a tremor shuddered its way through her body. Six years of separation had not gotten Shane Fortune out of her system. How could she ever hope to accomplish that now that he was back in her life?

"Penny for your thoughts."

Cynthia jumped at the sound of Shane's voice. "Uh…it's been a bit of a hectic day, that's all. I was just putting together in my mind what I needed to do in Phoenix."

"Mind if I join you?"

"It's your house." Her comment was uttered without expression.

He seated himself next to her, perhaps too close. "Did you get all your business in Tucson taken care of? Did everything go okay?"

"Yes, I think I'm closing in on the final leg of this mess.

After I take care of the Phoenix business, I should have everything wrapped up in another couple of days. Then I can…'' Her voice trailed off when she turned to look at him. The soft light played across his handsome features, evoking memories of a time when she believed she and Shane would be together forever.

A deep sorrow swept over her as the sadness lodged inside her. How could she possibly still love him after everything that had happened? Her throat tightened. She averted her gaze and swallowed to break the dryness. ''Uh…then I can concentrate on finding a place to live, so Bobby and I can get out of your hair and on with our lives. I'm sure you'll be glad to get your life back to normal.''

''Quite the contrary. I'm enjoying having you and Bobby here.'' He ran his fingertips lightly across the back of her hand, reveling in the softness of her skin and the tingle of excitement caused from just touching her. He covered her hand with his and dropped his voice to a low intimate level. ''You and Bobby are welcome to stay as long as you want.''

Her despair, her confusion, her anguish, her trepidation, her unrequited love—all her conflicting emotions exploded inside her. She couldn't keep them bottled up any longer. She jerked her hand away from his, shoved her chair back and jumped to her feet. She leveled a harsh look at him while trying to keep her real concerns and fears out of her voice. ''I don't know what's going on here or what you're trying to do with this solicitous act of yours and all the special attention to Bobby. Just what is it you're trying to prove? What's all this about?''

''Trying to prove?'' Her abrupt change of attitude caught Shane by surprise. ''I'm not trying to prove any-thing.'' It wasn't much of an answer, but it was the best he could come up with. He wasn't sure himself exactly what his motives were. He did know his thoughts and feelings about her were creating a monumental internal upheaval for him. Every time he saw her, his feelings deepened. But he had other priorities in his life—a life that didn't seem to have room for anyone else, regardless of his personal feelings. But it was a life that left him alone and lonely in the darkest hours of the night.

And then there was Bobby. He was a great little boy, one any man would be proud to call son—but what about his father? Shane recalled Cynthia's words about the difficulty of raising a child by herself and Bobby's comment about his father leaving before he was born. Yet the other thought about Bobby persisted—the one that had finally begun to take a definitive shape. As totally implausible as it sounded, could it be possible that he was Bobby's father? Their last few weeks together had been filled with the most intense passion he had ever experienced. It was almost as if he had been determined to store up enough of Cynthia McCree to last a lifetime. Another moment of sadness invaded his thoughts. He hadn't realized just how long that lifetime would be.

The boy appeared to be the age where he could have been conceived either right before he and Cynthia separated or immediately after. Every time he tried to talk to Cynthia about Bobby, he'd come up against an icy wall of resistance and a flat refusal to discuss Bobby in any detail. And if Bobby was his son... His thoughts trailed off. Surely Cynthia would have told him if she was pregnant with his child. Or would she? Had he hurt her so badly that she would have kept something this important to herself. He didn't know what to think or how to deal with that possibility, so he shoved it aside and returned his thoughts to Cynthia. He met the same icy wall when he kissed her, but not until after the heat and sensuality of her response told him the fire of passion still lived inside her—just as it did in him.

He touched her hair, then caressed her cheek. The feel of her skin sent a sensual warmth flowing through his body. His heartbeat quickened as he drank in her beauty. His words came out in a whisper and were the last thing he should have said at that moment and under those circumstances. "You make me breathe hard just looking at you."

She stepped away from his touch. Her terse response knocked him out of his moment of reverie. "Our problem was never in the bedroom." She furrowed her brow as she reflected on her words, her voice dropping to a near whisper. "At least I didn't think it was."

In a flash all the pain and hostility came flooding back. She leveled a hard look at him and blurted out her repressed anger. "But then, you never did me the courtesy of mentioning exactly what the problem was. You simply announced you didn't have any room in your life for me and walked out the door without once looking back."

Her irate words startled him. Again he spoke without thinking, as he tried to calm the pent-up emotions she'd hurled at him. "Maybe we could go back to where we left off and pick up the pieces." He knew as soon as he said it that he shouldn't have. It was the second time he'd blurted out the wrong thing.

She bristled. "Where we *left off* was with you walking out on me—not even a goodbye, let alone an explanation."

All the pain and humiliation of that horrible night flooded through her until there wasn't room for anything else. It ripped away softer thoughts of love and closeness and family. It had been the lowest point of her life, one she had tried for six years without success to bury in a place where it couldn't hurt her anymore.

She had to get away from him, from the memories and the shattered dreams—from a tempting nearness that she knew could easily be her downfall again. She turned and started to walk away from him, but broke into a run as she hurried through the den and up the stairs to her bedroom, shaken to the core by his comments and the stinging rush of raw emotion they produced.

Her inner turmoil ripped her apart. She wanted to be with Shane as much as she was afraid of what could happen. Agreeing to stay in his house had been a very bad idea. She needed to get out, to get away from him before it was too late. Her fear and trepidation broke out of the place where she had been trying so hard to contain it and came out in a rush of convulsive sobs.

Shane had remained motionless following Cynthia's abrupt departure from the patio. He was profoundly disturbed by the display of hurt her outburst had revealed. The worst part was knowing he was responsible for it. All these years it had bothered him, and now he'd come face-to-face with the full impact of the consequences of his selfish and callous actions.

He still didn't know how she would fit into his world, but he had finally been pushed into the realization that he didn't have a life without her. The dynamic, in-charge Shane Fortune found himself at a complete loss about what to do. He finally rose from his chair and went inside, closing and locking the door behind him. He turned out the lights and made his way through the dark house and up the stairs.

Her sobs grabbed his attention as he passed her door. The sound ripped at his heart. He had to do something, but he didn't know exactly what. He hesitated a moment, then knocked softly on her door. When he didn't receive an answer, he cautiously entered the room.

An overwhelming sense of guilt and sorrow twisted his

insides into knots the moment he saw her tearstained face and the pain in her eyes. He rushed across the room. "Cynthia… " He sat on the edge of her bed, put his arms around her and tried to pull her body against his. He wanted to provide her with some sort of comfort. He *needed* to provide her with some sort of comfort.

"Go away." The angry words came out between sobs as she struggled against his hold. "Just leave me alone."

"No." He refused to release her, holding her body even tighter against his. "I'm not going to leave you like this." He cradled her head against his shoulder and stroked her hair while rocking her in his arms. His anxiety level skyrocketed as he took on her emotional tumult in an effort to lessen her load. She finally stopped struggling and gradually succumbed to his insistent embrace. He placed a tender kiss on her forehead while continuing to hold her.

His emotion-laden words came out as a mere whisper. "I'm so sorry, Cynthia. I never meant to hurt you like this. It was such a difficult time for me. My life was in turmoil." He wasn't sure exactly where he was going with this, but he wanted to try to explain to her, to make her understand what had happened. And he wanted to seek her forgiveness.

"I knew what I wanted as a career. I'd always wanted to be a doctor, but beyond that I didn't have a clue. I didn't know where or how I fit into the scheme of things. Was I a Fortune or a Lightfoot? Which world was mine? Which culture was mine? I had a lot of anger and confusion in those days, and I wrongly took my frustrations out on you. I didn't understand how you could possibly be a part of my world when I didn't know what that world was or how I fit into it."

He kissed her forehead again. "For six years I've regretted what I said and what I did, and I've lived with the guilt and sorrow ever since then. I never meant to hurt you like this. I thought I was saving you from future hurt. Can you ever forgive me for what I did?''

Shane placed his fingertips beneath her chin and lifted her head until he could see her face. He kissed the tears away, tasting the saltiness. He lowered his mouth to hers, taking control before she had an opportunity to stop him.

The passion exploded the moment his lips touched hers. Cynthia heard his words and wanted to believe them, but did not know if she could trust them—or him. She was treading on thin ice. She needed to distance herself from him, but her willpower slipped away too quickly for her to keep hold of it. Almost as if someone else had control of her actions, she wrapped her arms around his neck and responded to his kiss.

His mouth demanded and she gave. Every bit of rapture that had ever been part of their past came rushing back at her full force. Once again she found herself enfolded in the security of Shane Fortune's arms, and she felt safe and happy.

Then reality set in.

''Please...leave.'' Her words may have had a breathless quality to them, but it was the result of fear, rather than physical arousal.

Shane hesitated a moment, not sure whether to continue his insistence that he stay or bow to her wishes. The sensual response of her kiss told him one thing, but the fear in her eyes and the pleading in her voice told him something quite different. He brushed a light kiss across her lips, rose to his feet and cast one last look of longing in her direction. The physical longing quickly combined with an emotional concern that surrounded his words with sincerity. ''Are you going to be all right?''

She nodded without saying anything.

''If you need anything...I'm just down the hall.'' Shane turned and left the room, even though he wasn't at all convinced he was doing the right thing.

Seven

"**I**s something wrong?" Cynthia was puzzled when she opened the front door and saw Isabelle's wrinkled brow. "You look worried. If you have some personal business to tend to, please let me know. I can certainly postpone my trip to Phoenix until another day."

"Oh, no, it's nothing like that. I was just wondering…" Isabelle nervously shifted her weight from one foot to the other. She glanced at the floor before looking up at Cynthia again. "Well, do you have a few minutes to help me with a couple of decisions about the wedding? I'd sure appreciate your input."

Cynthia smiled. "Of course. After you were so gracious to agree to watch Bobby for me, I'm pleased that I can return the favor." The two women settled themselves comfortably on the couch in the den. "Now, what can I do to help?" She attempted to put the obviously apprehensive young woman at ease. "Having never been married, I'm not sure how much help I'll be. But I'll give it my best shot.''

"It's, uh…'' Isabelle glanced uneasily at the floor again, rather than maintain eye contact.

Cynthia shifted her position on the couch as she realized the seriousness of Isabelle's as-yet-unspoken concerns. Whatever was on Isabelle's mind was obviously more than a simple matter of bridal etiquette, but she seemed reluctant to say what it was.

"I assure you, Isabelle, that anything you say to me will be kept in strictest confidence.''

"Well…I can't discuss this with my family, and I didn't know who else to turn to. I thought maybe, as someone who isn't involved in all this, you might have an unbiased perspective.''

"I'll do my best. What's troubling you?''

"It's, well…'' Then Isabelle blurted out the words as if she were thankful just to be rid of them. "It's just *everything*. It's the wedding, the marriage—but mostly it's Brad.''

"Do you love him?''

"I guess so…''

"You guess so?'' Cynthia arched an eyebrow and cocked her head. "Aren't you sure?'' She fixed Isabelle with a steady gaze. "Marriage is a big step and shouldn't be entered into unless you're really sure it's right. Are you having second thoughts about the wedding, or is it Brad that's causing you concern?''

"It's sort of all of it. For the past couple of weeks I've been trying to convince myself that I'm just getting cold feet about the wedding, that I'm just not ready for marriage. The truth is, it's not the wedding I'm concerned about—it's marrying Brad Rowan that worries me.''

"What do you think caused this change of heart?''

Isabelle scrunched up her face. "I'm not sure. I can't put my finger on exactly why the doubts happened or when they began. There are things going on that I don't know about—suspicious things, secrets that he's keeping from me. I ask and he denies. He says all the right things, but something is wrong. I can feel it as surely as I can feel the sun on my face when I walk outside, but I don't know what to do about it. The wedding plans are already so far along that it would be next to impossible to change the date. And to cancel it altogether...well, lots of people would be upset."

Cynthia digested Isabelle's words. This was far removed from what she'd anticipated. She carefully formulated her response. "If you have questions and doubts now, they won't simply go away by themselves with the passage of time. They'll grow until they become so huge that they bury you and the marriage. The doubts must be dealt with up front. It's your life and your future that's at stake. You can't allow the wishes and plans of other people to control your decision in something this important, something that will impact the rest of your life. You have to do what's best for you and not worry about whether someone will approve of your actions or someone else will be inconvenienced. I know that's very difficult to do, especially where family is concerned."

Cynthia gave Isabelle a warm smile. She adopted an upbeat tone of voice in an attempt to lighten the mood. "Was that more than you wanted to hear?"

Isabelle rose from the couch and offered a grateful smile in return. "No—it was exactly what I needed to hear. It certainly gives me something to think about." She glanced at her watch. "You'd better get started for Phoenix if you want to take care of your business and get back here before dark."

The words echoed in Cynthia's mind as she gathered her purse and car keys. *Doubts won't disappear with the passage of time. You have to do what's best for you regardless of what other people think.* But her own situation was different. Her decisions impacted an innocent boy's life. It was Bobby's welfare that had to come first.

Could he actually be Bobby's father?

Shane's turmoil had become so pervasive that it had cost him a night's sleep then interfered with his day's work. He attended a meeting, yet had no idea what had been discussed. He'd spent a good part of the day asking people to repeat what they'd just said because his mind had wandered to Cynthia and Bobby.

He had to do something. Things could not go on like that.

Had Cynthia purposely denied him knowledge of his son? He swallowed the lump in his throat but couldn't swallow the conflicting thoughts and feelings. He had to clear up that question. He had to find out the truth. But how? His current relationship with her was so tenuous he didn't think it would stand the strain of what could be a false accusation on his part. He needed to know the boy's exact date of birth. If he had that, then he wouldn't need to ask any questions.

He took a deep breath, then slowly expelled it. He could still taste her lips and feel the underlying passion they'd shared last night before she'd broken the kiss off. It had not been enough. It would never be enough. He had to do whatever was necessary to find out what the future held for the *three* of them. He pulled up to the garage and clicked the remote to open the door.

Shane entered the house through the kitchen and continued on toward the den. He immediately spotted Cynthia sitting in the recliner with her head back and her eyes closed. He saw the stress lines etched on her face. He wanted badly to be able to banish them, to take care of everything that had caused such a beautiful face to be marked with tension. But he was also aware that this *new* independent Cynthia would never allow it.

It was a perplexing problem. Everything had been so clear for him before he found her in his house late that night. Now nothing was clear. She'd done more than create sleepless nights and worrisome days for him. She'd forced him to rethink his life and what the future held. However, he was still left with the problem of how to confront her about Bobby.

He took a steadying breath and entered the den. His subdued voice barely carried across the room. "Are you asleep?"

His whispered words penetrated her foggy veil just before she succumbed completely to the drowsiness. She turned her head and slowly opened her eyes. "I'm afraid I almost dozed off. I suppose that means I should go upstairs rather than stay here." She stifled a yawn, then closed her eyes again.

He pulled an ottoman next to her chair and sat down. "You look tired. Did you have a rough day? Did you accomplish everything you needed to in Phoenix?"

"Yes."

He waited for her to continue, but no more words came from her. "Yes—what?"

"Yes, both—I had a rough day and took care of everything I needed to in Phoenix." She shifted her weight, opened her eyes and brought the recliner back to an upright position. She stifled another yawn. "It's been a nightmare of a problem, but the worst of it is behind me now. Just a few more details and then everything will be in order and I can close out the estate."

"You know what? I think you need a break. Tomorrow is one of my days to provide medical services on the reservation. Come with me. It will do you good to get away from the stress and pressure you've been under since you arrived."

"No... I couldn't do that. I—"

"Please?" He brushed his fingertips across her cheek, then took her hand in his. The words sprang from his mouth as a full-blown idea without his having given it any conscious thought. "I'd like very much to show you what prompted me to push for a children's hospital, why the need exists and the kind of work we'll be doing."

His persuasive voice, combined with the tantalizing sensation of his touch, wrapped her in a warm cocoon. All her resistance melted away. Perhaps she was just too tired to fight off the feeling, but try as she might, she could not find any reason to object to his plan. Quite the contrary— she sincerely wanted to know more about his work on the reservation, more about his special projects. He was definitely right about her needing a break from the stress, but would she be trading one type of stress for another in agreeing to spend the day with him? And there was Bobby. It would be an ideal way to introduce him to the Native American portion of his heritage.

"Well? I haven't heard an answer yet. Would you accompany me to the reservation tomorrow?"

"Does your invitation include Bobby?"

A warm smile curved up the corners of his mouth. "Of course it includes Bobby. Does that mean you'll go?"

"Well...it would be educational for Bobby." She returned his smile. "Yes, we'd like that."

"Good. We need to get an early start."

"In that case I'd better get myself out of this chair and

up to bed.'' As she rose to her feet, he jumped up and assisted her.

''I'll walk you to your door.''

He clasped her hand in his. The feel of her skin and the warmth of the contact sent a tremor of excitement through his body. They walked up the stairs together. When they reached her door, he leaned his face into hers and placed a soft kiss on her lips. ''I'll see you and Bobby in the morning. Good night, Cynthia.''

They lingered outside her door for a moment longer, his hand still clasping hers. The sensation was both comfortable and familiar, with neither of them putting forth an effort to terminate the contact. It was Cynthia who finally spoke.

''Well, I guess I'd better get to bed—'' she glanced shyly at the floor, then regained eye contact with him ''—if you'll give my hand back to me.''

He pulled her to him and said, his voice barely more than a whisper, ''If I have to.'' He released her hand, then enfolded her into his embrace. A moment later he captured her mouth with a sensual kiss that spoke of deeply felt emotions rather than lust—a kiss as soft as spring rain, yet conveying a strength to rival the mightiest storm.

Cynthia's blood coursed hotly through her veins. The soft intimacy rapidly built to intense fervor. Every fiber of truth in her being told her to put a stop to what was happening before it was too late, but she didn't want it to stop. It could only lead to trouble, but at that moment she didn't care. She encircled his neck with her arms. His heartbeat resonated with hers, as they pressed their bodies more tightly together. She felt his groan of pleasure as much as she heard it.

He was everything she'd ever wanted in a man, everything she needed. His tongue brushed hers, the textures meshing in a burst of shared excitement. His hands caressed her shoulders, her back, and finally cupped the firm roundness of her bottom. He pulled her hips tightly against his, the heat of his arousal increasing her ardor. Her insides quivered as she drew in a ragged breath. She threaded her fingers through his hair. Was there a chance for them, after all, or was it all physical on his part without any love?

A very shaken Cynthia jerked to attention as the reality of what was happening exploded in her head. She broke the delicious contact of their mouths. She stumbled backward a couple of steps and tried to get her ragged breathing under control. She'd sworn she would keep her distance from him and not allow herself once again to be drawn into his aura. All-out panic raced through her. In spite of all her intentions, she had been well on her way to making love with Shane. Their escalating excitement had to be brought back in check. Her wants, desires and needs must take second place to what was most important—protecting her son.

She touched trembling fingers to her kiss-swollen lips. The depth of Shane's passion glowed in his dark eyes, sending a tremor of renewed desire racing through her. It would be so easy for him to draw her back in. She fought to compose herself, to deny the temptation of Shane Fortune's nearness and his unmistakable allure.

He took her hand in his, kissed her palm, then held it against his chest. His heart beat strongly against her fingers. His voice contained a hint of huskiness. "What are you so afraid of, Cynthia? What is it that has you so scared?"

She quickly withdrew her hand from the warmth of his grasp. She put as much conviction into her words as she could. "I...I don't know what you're talking about."

"I can see it in your eyes. Whatever it is, I'd like to help."

"You're mistaken. Good night, Shane." She went into her bedroom and closed the door. Her heart pounded, only this time it was trepidation, rather than the sensual delight of Shane Fortune. She held her breath until she heard him walk away.

His words had more truth to them than he probably realized. She was definitely scared. Her most recent encounter with the all-too-tempting masculinity of Shane Fortune—or more accurately her total vulnerability where he was concerned—left her frightened to the core. She could not protect her son unless she was strong herself. She renewed her determination to do what needed to be done.

"I'm ready. Is it time to go yet?" Bobby's excitement spilled out as he looked expectantly at his mother. The drive from Chicago to Pueblo had turned him into a seasoned car traveler who knew what spending many hours on the road was all about. As soon as she told him of today's planned activities, he raced around the house gathering the things he wanted to take with him in the car.

Cynthia chuckled as she tried to slow down Bobby's excess energy. "We haven't had breakfast yet. Don't you think we should do that first?"

His expression fell. "Yeah…I guess so." He went into the kitchen and took his place at the table.

Shane set a glass of milk in front of him. "That will get you started, champ. Now, what do you want to eat?"

"I'm not hungry, Shane. Can we leave now?"

"I really think we need to have breakfast first. We have a busy and long day ahead of us, and we need to get fueled up."

Bobby looked at him, clearly in awe. "Are you going to have breakfast, too?"

Shane grinned. "I sure am. I think I'll have some scrambled eggs, ham and toast. How does that sound to you?"

Bobby grinned back at him as he squirmed in his chair, getting comfortable. "Yeah. Me, too. That's what I want."

Shane whirled toward the kitchen door. He'd seen Cynthia out of the corner of his eye as she stood in the doorway watching them. "What about you?" He cocked his head and shot her a questioning look. "Am I cooking for three?"

She quickly averted her gaze and headed for the coffeepot. "I suppose so—if it's not too much trouble." There was no question that Bobby idolized Shane. The knowledge tugged hard at her ever-increasing sense of guilt. If only she knew what was going on inside Shane's head, how he really felt about her. What he would do if he found out Bobby was his son. She took a swallow of coffee, hoping it would wash down her fear.

Shane gestured toward a chair. "It's no trouble at all. I'll get breakfast on the table, then we can be on our way."

"Yeah, Mommy, then we can be on our way." Bobby looked at Shane. "Right?"

"Right, champ."

Her son's imitation of Shane was not lost on Cynthia. And another layer of guilt attached itself to the rapidly growing lump that seemed to have found a permanent home in the pit of her stomach.

They made quick work of breakfast and were soon on their way to the reservation. Cynthia stared at the landscape as they traveled down the two-lane highway. She'd been so busy since her return to Pueblo, her mind occupied with the problems of her father's estate, that she had not taken the time to simply enjoy the scenery.

Shane kept up a descriptive commentary as he drove, pointing out various sights to Bobby. "You see that tall cactus? That's a giant saguaro, the symbol of this desert region. They can grow to be more than fifty feet tall." He glanced over his shoulder to Bobby in the back seat. "That's as high as a five-story building. Some of them live to be 250 years old. That flower blooming on the top is the state flower of Arizona."

Cynthia noted the fascination on Bobby's face. As long as Shane was imparting information, she decided it was a good time to introduce Bobby to a bit of his heritage in a setting where it wouldn't seem out of place. She turned toward Shane. "How large is the reservation? How many people live on it?"

Shane glanced at her, his expression showing his surprise at her question. "It's the second-largest reservation in the country. Its three parts total 2,854,789 acres, roughly the size of Connecticut. The reservation population is close to eight thousand. The tribal headquarters is located in the town of Sells, which is where we're headed."

They drove onto the reservation. Cynthia noted that only a small roadside sign announced that they had crossed the boundary and entered tribal land. Shane continued to provide a travelogue. He pointed out the Kitt Peak Observatory, with its large white domes where a total of nineteen telescopes of various types and sizes were stationed. "And over there is Baboquivari Peak. At 7,730 feet it's the highest point on the reservation. It's also home to the ancient gods and is considered sacred."

Cynthia continued to stare out the window at the wide open spaces that stretched for miles without any sign of habitation. "I've never been on the reservation before. Is all of it this…sparse? There was that one small convenience store with the art gallery next door a little way inside the reservation, but other than that, I haven't seen even a gas station. How large is Sells?''

"The Tohono O'odham don't discourage tourism, but they don't exactly encourage it, either. You won't find motels, plentiful gas stations or even public camping facilities. Sells has a population of a little under three thousand people and is the largest town on the reservation.''

They arrived at the tribal headquarters and were greeted by tribal leaders. After Shane introduced Cynthia and Bobby, the men discussed business. Cynthia took a book from her purse and found a comfortable chair. Bobby wandered around the large room, carefully inspecting the baskets and pieces of pottery. He was particularly fascinated by a puzzlelike drawing.

He carried it over to Cynthia. "What's this, Mommy?''

She took it from his hand. "I'm not sure. It says, 'Man in the Maze.''' She studied the circular pattern for a moment. "This figure must be the man, and he needs to find his way through this maze.'' She started to trace one of the many routes within the circle.

"But where is the man trying to go?''

"I don't know, Bobby. Let's see if this is for sale. If it is, then we can take it back to Shane's house with us. I'll bet he can explain it to you.'' She carried the drawing to the counter and made the purchase.

Shane motioned to Cynthia and Bobby. "Let's get going. Today's visiting-doctor station is a little village about twenty miles from here.''

They arrived at the designated location to find several people already waiting for the doctor. Shane grabbed two large bags from his Ford Explorer and proceeded immediately to a back room to set up. He glanced at all the anxious faces, then turned to Cynthia. "Could you explain that it will take me a few minutes to get ready?''

"Sure. You go ahead." She turned to face the assembled people, mostly mothers with children. She quickly and efficiently organized as much as she could. She made a list of names and ages of patients and their reason for seeing the doctor, along with any symptoms they described.

Even Bobby helped. Without asking his mother or even telling her what he was going to do, he went to the car and retrieved the toys and games he'd brought with him. He offered them to the children to play with while they were waiting.

Cynthia blinked away the tears misting over her eyes as she choked back a sob. She had never been prouder of him than she was at that moment. Turning toward the door to the back room, she saw Shane standing there watching the proceedings. She didn't know how long he'd been watching, but the expression on his face said he'd seen enough to know what had happened. His look exuded warmth, but his eyes showed something that sent a little shiver of apprehension through her—a tender fondness and pride directed toward Bobby.

Shane collected his thoughts and quickly became all business. "Well, shall we get started?" He set a clipboard on the table. "I'd like for everyone to sign—"

"Is this what you need?" Cynthia handed him the list she'd made, noting the surprise that covered his features as he scanned it.

He gave her a warm smile that quickly turned into a teasing grin. "Yes, Assistant Cynthia, I believe this is exactly what I need. Thank you."

The day passed quickly with the two of them working efficiently as a team. They managed a half-hour break to eat the lunch she'd packed, then resumed tending to the constant stream of patients. By late afternoon everyone had been seen by the doctor. Shane repacked his two bags and carried them out to the car while Cynthia helped Bobby gather his toys and games.

"I was real proud of you today, Bobby." She kissed him on the cheek. "That was good of you to share your toys with the other boys and girls."

"I was real proud of you, too, champ. That was a very nice gesture." Shane crossed the room from the front door and knelt to help gather the toys.

He turned to Cynthia. "And I want to thank you for all your help, too. By stepping in and organizing the waiting room and lining everything up for me, you made it possible for me to see more patients." His voice dropped to a seductive level. He leaned so close to her she could feel his breath tickling her cheek as he spoke. "We work well together, don't you think?"

His words sent a little shiver across the back of her neck. She tried to respond in a businesslike manner. "I'm glad I was able to be of some help to you." Excitement tingled through her body. Part of it was due to the nearness of the very sexy Shane Fortune. But not all of it.

She had been witness to a different facet of this dynamic man during the course of the day—a compassionate and caring doctor with a genuine dedication to his patients, especially the children. It touched her heart. It also left her even more unsettled and guilty about keeping Bobby's identity from him, but she knew it was best for all concerned—at least she thought she knew it.

She stood up and surveyed the room. "I think that's everything."

Shane took the box of toys from her. "I'll carry these. I need to stop in Sells for a few minutes, then we're through for the day."

They drove to the tribal office, and Shane quickly concluded his business while Cynthia and Bobby waited in the car. Bobby was tired but refused to give in to it. He'd been going at a high energy level all day. The drive back to Pueblo, Cynthia hoped, would provide him with an opportunity to calm down. He'd probably go to sleep as soon as he had his dinner.

Shane opened the door and slid in behind the steering wheel. "I'm starved. How about the two of you? Let's say we find a restaurant and get something to eat."

Bobby piped up from the back seat, "Yeah, I'm hungry."

Cynthia added her vote. "I could use something to eat, too."

Shane shifted the car into gear. "Dinner it is." He took the same two-lane highway off the reservation and soon came upon a roadside diner. "I've eaten here several times. It doesn't look like much from the outside, but the food is good."

They made quick work of dinner and were soon back on the road. Cynthia turned around to check on Bobby. "Just as I thought—he's sound asleep. It's been a long day for him."

Shane reached over and touched her cheek, then covered her hand with his. "How about you? Are you exhausted? I'd like to take a quick detour by the Children's Hospital construction site. It's right on the way and I want to show you what we're doing."

"Well…" Although the day had been comfortable, she wasn't sure what to do or say. She should have been on alert, on her guard to stave off anything that would resurrect the intimate closeness that once existed between them. She *should* have been…

"I'd very much like to hear more about your hospital project."

The warm sensuality flowed from his touch through her body, spreading to every corner of her consciousness. Regardless of her intentions, the magic of Shane Fortune had worked its way back into her life. To try to convince herself otherwise would be futile.

Her logic tried to tell her one thing, but her emotions told her something quite different. Spending the day with Shane, the two of them working together to give something to the community, it all felt so very right. It was one of her reasons for moving back to Pueblo, even though she had not figured out exactly where her services could be the most effective. But today had given her insight into how she could give to the community. Surprisingly it was not through her career as an attorney as she'd assumed, but rather by working with Shane.

Should she share those thoughts with him? What kind of message would that send him? And if she was willing to take a chance on opening her life to include him again, what did that do to her decision to keep Bobby's identity from him?

Eight

The entire day had been an eye-opening experience for him and had answered many of his worries, Shane thought as he steered the Explorer to the office trailer next to the construction site. He had been so certain she would not fit in to the path he'd chosen that he'd never asked himself what part she could play in the greater scheme. Instead, she'd pitched in and efficiently organized things. She'd truly been an asset.

She had fit very easily and comfortably into the life he had designed for himself and also seemed genuinely interested in the hospital project. He showed her the blueprints for the hospital and explained the type of services they intended to provide for the various Native American communities in the area.

They left the trailer and wandered toward the construction. He laced their fingers together as they walked. "That—" he pointed to the workmen's elevator in front of them "—is where Mike Dodd was killed." He felt the tremor that swept through her body as he continued to hold her hand.

"How's the investigation coming along?"

Shane's brow furrowed as he slowly shook his head. "Not good. Every time I talk to someone, it's my brother Riley's name that comes back to me. I've heard it over and over. Riley and Mike Dodd didn't like each other. Riley was at the construction site the day before the murder and also that day, two days in a row, when he normally wouldn't be there more than a couple of times a month. Riley and Mike were overheard having an angry argument in the office trailer the day before Mike's death. Riley's fingerprints were found inside the elevator. Each thing is easily explainable by itself, but you put them all together and it doesn't look good."

Cynthia gave his hand a comforting squeeze. "I'm sure it will all work out okay. If Riley is innocent, he doesn't—"

"*If* Riley is innocent?" Shane cocked his head and stared at her for a moment as if he hadn't heard her correctly. "Of course he's innocent."

"I'm sorry. I didn't mean to imply otherwise."

He let out a sigh of resignation and with it some of his exasperation. "I know you didn't. This whole thing really has me upset. It's almost like someone had gone out of their way to make it appear that he did it, and as near as I can tell, Riley doesn't seem to be taking it very seriously."

"Well, you have to admit that Riley certainly added fuel to that fire when he spent the night with Mike's sister, Angelica."

"He did what?" Shane's eyes grew wide with shock. His words were a combination of anger and incredulity. "What are you talking about?"

Cynthia frowned in confusion. "Riley spent the night following the funeral with Angelica. What's the matter? You seem angry. I assumed this was old news."

"*Old* news? Not hardly. This is the first I've heard of it." He clenched his jaw into tight lines, as if fighting to keep his displeasure under control. "Where did you hear such a pack of lies?"

"Pack of lies?" His reaction puzzled her. She shook her head as her confusion increased. "I heard it from Isabelle. She mentioned it when we were talking yesterday morning before I went to Phoenix. She didn't say anything about it being some sort of a secret. I just assumed you knew about it."

"Isabelle told you? Where the hell did she hear something like that? Certainly not from Riley."

"She said Brad told her—" she could not keep the hint of irritation out of her voice "—and before you ask me, no, I don't know who told him or how he knew."

His voice so low that she had to strain to hear him, Shane muttered, "Brad. That figures."

She looked at him questioningly. "I don't understand…"

He took a calming breath, then squeezed her hand and offered an apologetic smile. "I'm sorry, I didn't mean to snap at you. It's just that you caught me by surprise with that little tidbit. Forgive me?"

She returned his smile as relief settled over her. "Sure."

They stayed a few minutes longer, then returned to the car. Before they could drive away, the security guard came by on his rounds. Shane and the guard exchanged a couple of minutes of conversation, then he pulled out onto the road.

The closeness that developed over the course of the day had intensified during their visit to the construction site. It continued to fill the car as they drove back to Pueblo. They talked quietly about the day's events, discussing the various cases that Shane handled. She'd seen in him a different man from the one she'd known six years ago—the one who'd broken her heart. This man was compassionate, caring and gentle. This man would be easy for any woman to love. Was she fooling herself into believing what she wanted, rather than seeing what was real? It was a disturbing question without a ready answer, but one she didn't shove aside.

They arrived back at Shane's house well after dark. Cynthia unfastened Bobby from the car seat.

"I really hate to wake him, but he's too big for me to carry anymore."

"Don't wake him." Shane lifted the sleeping boy out of the car and carried him into the house. It all felt very comfortable, just like a real family. His suspicions about Bobby had continued to poke at his consciousness, growing stronger with every time they passed through his mind. He needed to find a way to the truth without upsetting the still-fragile renewal of his relationship with Cynthia.

He carried Bobby up the stairs and into the bedroom. A few minutes later the little boy was tucked in bed without once waking up.

Cynthia kept her voice at a whisper as she watched her sleeping son. "He really wore himself out today. It's been a long time since I've been able to get him to take a nap, though he always has an hour or so of quiet time after lunch. That didn't happen today."

Shane put his arm around her shoulders as they left Bobby's bedroom, closing the door behind them. "He's a terrific little boy. He was certainly generous in sharing his toys."

"Bobby has always been very generous and giving, but

I have to admit that it did surprise me that he jumped in so quickly to do that.'' She allowed a loving smile to turn up the corners of her mouth. "I was proud of him today. He's growing up so fast. It seems just yesterday that I could hold him in my arms and now…'' The many loving memories of raising her son replaced her words.

They walked down the hallway, neither of them saying anything as they passed her bedroom and continued on. He stopped at the door to his bedroom and pulled her into his arms. He caressed her shoulders as he held her body tightly against his. A contented sigh made its way out of his mouth. He brushed a gentle kiss across her cheek, then whispered in her ear, "You have no idea how much I've missed you.''

The warmth of his embrace made her feel safe and secure. And at the same time his body pressing against hers sent a heated jolt of desire shooting through her. It was the moment of truth. She knew exactly what she was doing.

His mouth came down on hers, chasing away the last shred of logic clinging to her senses. Passions she was sure she had safely tucked away exploded with a force that truly shocked her. His tongue brushed against hers, igniting her ardor further and leaving nothing held back. Her body had not been this alive since the last time Shane made love to her all those years ago. She put her arms around his neck, eagerly welcoming his attentions.

The blood surged hot and fast through her veins, touching every part of her being. There would be no turning back, no playing it safe by putting a stop to what was happening before it was too late. It was already too late. There wasn't room for even a breath of air to pass between their bodies, yet he still managed to pull her even closer. Her ragged breathing matched his, each breath drawing her nearer to the moment she craved, to the moment they would again be joined together as one.

She ran her fingers through his hair, then over the back of his shirt. Every sensation, every nuance, every thrill that had ever been part of their lovemaking exploded inside her. She worked her hands beneath his shirt, skimming her fingers across the bare skin of his muscular back. A groan of desire rumbled from deep inside his chest, resonating with her need as insistently as his kiss.

He released his control of her mouth. His husky words tickled across her ear. "Oh, Cynthia...you are the most incredible, the most desirable—" His mouth came down on hers again. His hands slid across her back, then cupped the roundness of her bottom and pulled her hips against his. She could not stop the little moan of pleasure that escaped her throat, nor could she ignore the evidence of his arousal pressing against her.

He twined his tongue with hers, eagerly reacquainting himself with her unique and addictive taste. It hadn't been that long ago that he'd believed he would never again hold her in his arms or feel the heat of her passion. Every inch of his body ached for her touch. He was afraid to release her for fear she would slip away from him. So he scooped her up in his arms and carried her into his bedroom, pushing the door shut with his foot. He set her down on her feet next to his bed.

Shane yanked his shirt over his head and dropped it on the floor, then kicked off his shoes. He fought to bring his ragged gasps under control. His hands framed her lovely face. Passion burned in the depths of her blue eyes, exciting him so much he could barely get out his words. "If you don't want this, please tell me now while I still have a thread of control left."

She responded by sliding her hands across his bare

chest. A low groan of pleasure escaped his throat. Pieces of clothing dropped to the floor as a heightened sense of urgency filled the air. A minute later they were wrapped in each other's arms on the expanse of his king-size bed.

He captured her mouth with a hungry kiss that demanded as much as it gave. His fingertips skimmed down the side of her neck, over the curve of her shoulder, then across the swell of her breast. Each touch of her silky skin inflamed his already highly stimulated senses, sending a bolt of intense desire through his body. He kissed behind her ear, then trailed the tip of his tongue from the base of her throat to the pebbled texture of her taut nipple. Her labored breathing matched his as he drew the puckered treat into his mouth and gently suckled.

His hand found its way to the sensitive skin of her inner thighs. His fingers grazed the downy softness nestled between her legs, then parted the folds and entered the moist heat of her femininity. Her soft moan sent little waves of ecstasy rippling through his belly. Hers was a body he had once known intimately—every secret place that excited her, every nuance of her response to his stimulation. And now as he discovered everything anew, he found her even more exciting than before.

He released her nipple from his mouth, then teased the other one with his tongue before eagerly capturing it. A jolt of electricity shot through him the moment her fingers came in contact with his hardened manhood. He wanted their lovemaking to last the entire night, but knew he couldn't hold out much longer against the provocative sensation of her touch and the feel of her bare skin.

The moment she stroked his rigid manhood, a tingling sensation ran up her arm and invaded her entire body. Cynthia arched her back, urging him to an increased fervor. Her hips rose and fell of their own accord against the searing intensity of his expert touch. She gasped for air as he played her body with the expertise of a virtuoso capable of obtaining the ultimate in perfection. The previous six years disappeared in an incendiary flash of ecstasy as if they had never been apart. No one had ever been able to excite her in the same way Shane Fortune had.

His mouth moved from her nipple to the side of her neck, then his tongue thrust aggressively against hers. His hand pushed hard against her womanhood as burning need ripped through her body. She wanted still more.

Shane pulled back from her just long enough to reach for the nightstand drawer and withdraw the condom packet. He ripped it open and a few moments later settled his body between her thighs. His words came out in ragged gasps. "You are the most exquisite… I can't even think straight around you." He ran his hands up her rib cage until he could cup her breasts. He placed a kiss between them, then another on her stomach.

The tickle of his hot breath across her skin was followed by the enticing sensation of his lips on her inner thighs. She quivered in anticipation, then he finally placed the most intimate kiss of all at the very core of her womanhood. Every nerve ending in her body screamed out for the ultimate fulfillment.

He thrust forward ever so slowly until his entire length was inside her. A hard groan bordering somewhere between pleasure and ecstasy caught in his throat when her heated folds closed around his hardness. He set a smooth rhythm that escalated much more quickly than he wanted it to.

They moved together in unison, a sexual compatibility they had once shared through many nights of making love. Everything was so familiar yet had a delicious new level of excitement that exploded around them like an out-of-control fire.

She wrapped her arms and legs tightly around his body and squeezed her eyes shut. The convulsions started deep inside her and quickly spread. "Shane, I—" Her whispered words stuck in her throat, then were cut off completely when his mouth found hers. He gave one final deep thrust. She felt him shudder as the hard spasms rippled through his body.

She clung to him as if he were life itself. Her exhilaration soared, leaving her physically drained yet enveloped in a cloud of euphoria. She snuggled in the warm protection of his embrace. She loved him so much, though it was something she'd tried so hard to deny. She always had and she always would. The only thing that could make the moment even better would be Shane saying he loved her. He'd never once told her that during all the time they'd been together, and she longed to hear it.

The security of his arms, the sound of his heartbeat as she rested her head against his damp chest, what she had seen that day of his dedication to his beliefs and convictions—everything about him conveyed strength and purpose. The last man she made love with had been Shane Fortune, and that was six years ago. No one she'd met in the interim had even grabbed her interest, let alone captured her passion. There'd been no one in her life other than Shane. And then there was her son—*their* son. Had she betrayed the secure environment she'd created for Bobby by giving in to her own desires? It was a question that did not have an easy answer, and she feared it might haunt her in the future.

Her euphoria was short-lived when the sobering light of reality brought her back down to earth. It was a bittersweet moment. Now more than ever she needed to resolve her turmoil about whether to divulge Bobby's true identity to Shane. If only she knew how he really felt, whether or not he loved her. And whether her closest secret would cost her any love he felt.

Cynthia stared at the glowing numbers on the digital clock—four-thirty in the morning. She turned to look at Shane, being careful not to disturb him. She'd been afraid to move for fear of waking him, so she'd lain awake for fifteen minutes trying in vain to make sense of what had happened. She cautiously slipped out of his bed, gathered her clothes and retreated down the hall to her bedroom.

A shiver made its way through her body. One thing was for certain—if there had ever been any hope of getting Shane out of her system, she had destroyed it the moment she'd allowed him to lead her into his bedroom. She was sinking into a quagmire of conflicting desires and fears. A small sob caught in her throat. And at the center of it all was her need to protect her son.

She climbed into her own bed, but was unable to get back to sleep. Too many thoughts and images circulated through her mind. If she did tell Shane about Bobby, how should she do it, especially in light of their having made love? She certainly couldn't just blurt it out as if it was something that had previously slipped her mind and she'd suddenly remembered it.

The exact nature of her fears had shifted dramatically over the past couple of days. She had observed the growing closeness between Bobby and Shane with ever-increasing anxiety. She'd come to believe that Shane would not reject the boy. But her new and larger concern far overshadowed that. She feared Shane's affection for Bobby might lead him to try to get custody of her son, especially if he was angry about her not having told him he was a father.

Would he use her son as a means of getting back at her? Could the compassionate and caring man she'd spent the day with yesterday do something so terrible? A wave of fear made her physically flinch. The man she loved attempting to take her son away from her...

A single tear made its way down her cheek as the sorrow combined with her fear settled inside her. She knew she would never be able to survive something that horrible. Shane hadn't said anything to her about love or commitment or the future. Without that she could not risk her son's security and well-being. With single-minded determination she reinforced her vow to keep Bobby's identity a secret.

She took a deep breath and tried to settle the anxiety running unchecked through her body. She had an appointment that morning, the last step in settling her father's estate. Then she could start looking for a house for Bobby and her. She got out of bed, showered and dressed, then went downstairs.

Before she'd emotionally prepared herself, Shane wandered out of the kitchen carrying a cup of coffee. Wariness clung to his words. "I missed you this morning. I woke up and reached for you, but you weren't there."

A shiver of trepidation darted across the back of her neck. She reached to still it while glancing nervously at the floor. "I...I thought it would be better for me to return to my own room...in case Bobby awoke early."

"I see. I thought for a minute there might have been a problem."

"Well—" she swallowed her nervousness "—now that you mention it, I think we were far too hasty last night...caught up in a moment that should not have been."

He arched an eyebrow, cocked his head and looked at her questioningly. "What do you mean?"

"I mean—" she gathered her strength and determination while forcing a firm control to her voice "—it was a mistake and never should have happened. Things were over between us six years ago. It's to no one's benefit to resurrect something based solely on a misplaced physical attraction." She turned away from him, knowing her blatant lie must have shown on her face. It had been far more than merely physical desires—at least for her.

He grabbed her arm and turned her around so he could see her. Urgency surrounded his words. "What are you talking about? There was no mistake about last night."

"You're wrong." Her words were uttered with confidence and finality, but inside she was running scared.

He held on to her arm until she worked it free of his grasp. He saw the fear in her eyes and decided not to pursue it at that moment. It was a fear he'd seen many times since her arrival, but now he was beginning to understand it. It had to do with Bobby. Every new piece of the puzzle pointed toward Bobby being his son. He needed answers, but he knew he had to be careful in how he went about getting them.

"Isabelle was gracious enough to volunteer a couple of hours of her time this morning, and she'll be here soon. I want to get Bobby up and dressed before she arrives. I should be finished with my meeting by ten o'clock. If all goes well, this will be the final step. I'll be able to file all the papers and close out the estate." She turned away from him again before he could say anything.

He watched her climb the stairs. *Isabelle may be arriving soon, but she will be leaving far sooner than you think.* He had made his decision. He planned to spend the day alone with Bobby and this time, unlike when the two of them spent the afternoon in the pool, he would not be afraid to ask Bobby questions about his father.

Isabelle arrived about half an hour later. Cynthia picked up her file, kissed Bobby goodbye and left for her appointment.

Shane watched from the living-room window as she drove down the street, then he called to Isabelle. "I have a really light schedule today, just a few things this afternoon. Why don't you run along and take care of your own business matters, and I'll stay here with Bobby."

Isabelle glanced questioningly at her brother. "Are you sure you don't mind?"

He gave her a reassuring smile. "I don't mind at all."

Shane was very pleased with himself as he watched Isabelle's car back out of the driveway. He turned toward Bobby. "How would you like to go on an adventure today?"

Bobby looked up at him curiously. "An adventure? What kind?"

"Well—" he steered the little boy toward the garage door "—how about a trip to the Native American tourist center, then the museum? We can have lunch in the park and go see some horses after that. How does that sound to you?"

A grin spread across Bobby's face. "That sounds neat!"

Bobby's enthusiasm for everything new was infectious. Shane found himself seeing things in an exciting new light as he introduced Bobby to a world the little boy had never seen before. Shane showed him the intricate basket weaving and designs of the Tohono O'odham tribe. Bobby spotted the same drawing of a maze that Cynthia had purchased on the reservation.

He pointed to it. "What does that mean?"

"That's the Man in the Maze. It represents the journey

of man. He starts at the top when he's born and moves through all the turns and changes as he acquires knowledge, strength and understanding, until he reaches the end where he reflects on the wisdom he has gained during his life.''

Bobby's eyes opened wide in amazement. "Gosh."

From the museum they went to the park where Shane bought lunch from a hot-dog vendor. They took their food to a nearby picnic table. After they finished eating, Shane bought some peanuts and they sat on a park bench feeding the squirrels. He took a calming breath and finally asked the questions that had been on his mind all day.

"Did your mommy ever tell you anything about your daddy?"

Bobby threw some peanuts on the ground and laughed when the squirrels scrambled to grab them away from the birds. "Only that he went away."

"Do you know where he went or why he had to go away?"

Bobby frowned and squirmed on the bench, as if uncomfortable with the conversation. "I don't know." He looked up at Shane, his eyes filled with the type of honesty only a child could produce. "I wish I had a daddy."

The raw emotion of the moment tore at Shane's heart and almost destroyed his composure. Then Bobby told him something that left him totally unnerved and nearly took his breath away.

"My middle name's Shane, just like yours." Then he repeated it, his chest puffed out with pride. "My name's Robert Shane McCree, and I'm five and a half years old."

"Five and a *half*..." Shane gulped down the spiraling emotion that lodged in his throat and tried to calm the churning in his stomach. That half year made all the difference in the world. He tried to sound casual, not wanting to add any unspoken implication to his words. "I didn't realize you were that old. When is your birthday?" He held his breath as he listened to Bobby's answer.

He didn't know what to think or how he felt as his suspicions were finally confirmed. This little boy, this captivating child any man would be proud to call his son, was his son—his and Cynthia's. It was probably the most sobering news of his life. The only thing that came close was his belated realization of the colossal blunder he'd made when he'd cut Cynthia out of his life.

Shane's mind turned back to the last couple of weeks when he and Cynthia were together. He had already made the decision to break it off with her. That night doubts began to set in. In a totally spontaneous moment they had made love on the patio of his house late at night. He had been so torn between his decision to terminate their affair and the very intense physical passion that had overwhelmed him that he had neglected to take proper precautions. Two weeks later he had finally broken off their relationship. That had to have been the night Bobby was conceived.

The joy and elation that had exploded inside him was quickly overtaken by feelings of betrayal, and anger at Cynthia for keeping his son a secret from him. This was something much bigger than hurt feelings from years ago. The pain knotted in his stomach. How could she have done this to him? Especially after they'd made love last night with all that long-suppressed passion.

He knew he had to confront her with his suspicions about Bobby that evening. It could not be put off any longer. He wasn't sure how to approach her, but he knew he needed to handle it carefully. He wouldn't gain anything by going into it with an outward display of anger, and he didn't want to do something that would make

Cynthia take Bobby and leave Pueblo. He didn't want to take a chance on upsetting Bobby, either. This little boy certainly wasn't to blame. He—

"Shane?" Bobby's impatient tugging on his shirtsleeve made him realize that the little boy had been talking to him. "Can we, Shane?"

"I'm sorry, champ. What did you say?"

"Can we go look at the horses now?"

Shane smiled at the endearing sight of the eager young face. Emotion welled up inside him as he took Bobby's hand, only this time he was certain it was his son's hand he clasped. "You bet we can."

Cynthia hurried up the walkway to the front door. An uneasiness pricked at her, a tremor of apprehension telling her that something was wrong. Isabelle's car was gone. Perhaps she and Bobby had gone to the store, or maybe she'd taken him to a movie, although neither possibility struck her as likely.

As soon as she entered the quiet house, it was obvious they weren't there. Isabelle had known Cynthia was only going to be gone for a couple of hours. There was no reason for her to have taken Bobby anywhere. She searched for a note, anything to tell her what had happened. After finding nothing, she attempted to reach Isabelle on the phone.

The sick feeling churned in the pit of her stomach as she listened to Isabelle's explanation about Shane insisting that he would watch Bobby. She knew as surely as she knew the sun rose in the east and set in the west that he had discovered the truth. One thing was certain—whatever happened between Shane and her had to be kept away from Bobby. She would not allow her son to be an innocent pawn. She prayed that Shane had not said anything to Bobby, that he could understand and honor that need.

The rest of Cynthia's day turned into a muddled and distraught collection of disconnected thoughts and wasted efforts. Each passing hour doubled her tension, and the stress churned inside her to the point where she felt she'd actually be sick.

At last the kitchen door opened and Bobby charged in from the garage, bubbling over with excitement. "Hi, Mommy! You should have been with Shane and me. We had a whole bunch of fun!"

She nervously glanced at Shane. She didn't know how to read the expression on his face. It was as if he'd put on a mask and was hiding behind it. Her anxiety level jumped even higher, if that was possible. She quickly returned her attention to Bobby before Shane could say anything. She forced an outer calm. "I was surprised when I got back and you weren't here." She extended a confident smile and tried to keep the concern out of her voice. "What did the two of you do all day?"

Bobby kept up a constant line of chatter for what remained of the afternoon, all through dinner and into the evening. Just as the day before, he had gone at full speed without resting and had exhausted himself but didn't want to stop. She was finally able to get him to bed.

As she tucked him in, a shiver of trepidation moved through her body. She knew without looking that Shane was responsible, that he was standing in the doorway watching her. Feeling her apprehension rise, she didn't dare turn around to look at him. She kissed Bobby on the cheek.

"Mommy?" He looked up at her, his expression very serious.

"Yes, honey?" Another tremor darted through her body.

"I wish Shane could be my daddy."

Cynthia sat in stunned silence. Every bit of sanity and reason surrounding her life sank into the bottomless pit of her stomach. She didn't know what to say or do. She desperately fought back tears. Her throat went dry. She finally managed a weak smile and said, "It's late. You should be asleep."

Her entire body went numb, then the anguish flooded her. A sick feeling tried to work its way up her throat. She felt as if she'd been kicked in the stomach and had all the breath knocked out of her. She could not stop the involuntary action that made her turn around toward Shane. He cocked his head and shot her an odd look, one she didn't know how to interpret.

All-out panic crashed through her body as she fought back the tidal wave of emotion. A dull ache throbbed at her temples. She continued to sit on the edge of Bobby's bed, afraid to leave the room. She knew she would have to face Shane with the truth—a truth he must surely know by now.

The ringing doorbell gave her a welcome respite. The unavoidable moment of truth had been put on hold. Shane leveled one last questioning look at her, then went downstairs to answer the door.

Cynthia hurried to the top of the stairs. She recognized the caller—Riley, Shane's brother. This delay did not change what she knew to be inevitable. It was no longer a matter of whether she should tell Shane about his son. Now she would have to explain why she'd kept Bobby's identity from him. Ropes of anguish knotted in her stomach. The situation had gone from bad to worse.

Nine

The two men went to the den, where Shane poured each of them a drink. He handed a glass to Riley. "So what brings you by?"

"I hadn't seen you for a while, that's all. I thought I'd stop by and see how things are going."

"Things are going fine. Thanks for asking." Shane studied his brother for a moment. Riley tried to put on an air of indifference, as if nothing bothered him, but Shane saw beneath the facade. "Now that the pleasantries are out of the way, why don't you tell me the real purpose of your visit?"

Riley's anger flared for a brief instant. "Can't you cut me a little slack?" He quickly regained his composure. "I didn't want anything special. I just happened to be in the neighborhood and saw your lights on." He took a swallow of his drink. "I, uh, was just wondering if you'd heard anything new about Link Templeton's investigation."

"Nothing *official* in the last day or two." Cynthia's

words returned to Shane about Riley having spent the night
with Angelica Dodd. He'd started to ask Isabelle about it,
but had decided against it. The same question reared its
head with Riley, but again he decided against pursuing
such a ridiculous line of questioning. It couldn't be anything more than stupid gossip. He clenched and un-
clenched his jaw. Any kind of information that had come
from Brad Rowan wasn't worth the time it took to repeat
it. Besides, Link was a fair and honest man. He wouldn't
be taken in by malicious gossip. "How about you? Anything new?"

"Same here. For a while there it seemed like every time
I turned around, he was finding something else to connect
me to it." Riley chuckled nervously. "He's obviously
come to his senses, realized that I couldn't have done it
and turned his snooping in other directions."

Shane's voice carried the ominous overtones that fit his
feelings in the matter. "*I* know you're innocent, but you'd
better take Link's investigation seriously. He's turned up
quite a bit of circumstantial evidence connecting you to
the murder."

"Yeah, but that's all it is—circumstantial. He doesn't
have anything *real*."

"Dammit, Riley! You'd better start taking this seriously
before you end up in jail."

Riley responded to Shane's outburst with a nervous
chuckle. "How can I possibly take it seriously when it's
so ludicrous? He's just blowing smoke. He doesn't have
any hard evidence."

Shane scowled at him. "We'll see if you're still laughing when Link shows up at your door with a warrant for
your arrest." Shane firmly believed Riley would never be
arrested, certainly not on a few pieces of flimsy circumstantial evidence, but he felt compelled to try to drive

home once again the seriousness of the matter. He raised his voice. "You've got to treat this with more respect!"

Shane's angry voice carried upstairs, but Cynthia could not make out the words. Whatever he and Riley were arguing about, it couldn't involve her. If she was lucky, it might even divert Shane's attention away from her—and Bobby. She started to go to the kitchen to get a glass of iced tea, then decided to wait as she tried to determine whether Shane and Riley were still involved in a heated discussion. After five minutes of not hearing any angry voices, she cautiously ventured down the stairs.

Shane and Riley emerged from the den just as Cynthia reached the kitchen door. Shane called to her, his voice sounding upbeat, rather than angry.

"Cynthia, I'm taking Riley and Isabelle to dinner tomorrow night, just a quiet little family get-together that's long overdue. I'd like for you and Bobby to join us."

A *family* get-together—the words were not lost on her. Neither was the knowing expression on Shane's face. An uncomfortable level of anxiety tried to take hold, leaving her insides quivering with trepidation over what he was really saying. She forced down her rising apprehension, determined to present a strong outer persona. "I, uh, thank you for the invitation, but I'm afraid I won't be able to."

"I hope you can rearrange your schedule and join us, Cynthia," Riley said. He glanced at his watch, then turned his attention to Shane. "I need to get going."

Cynthia took advantage of the change in direction of the conversation and went into the kitchen. She poured herself a glass of iced tea, intending to take it back to her bedroom. She breathed a sigh of relief when she peered around the corner into the foyer and didn't see Shane anywhere.

A little of the anxiety drained from her body. She hurried toward the staircase, but didn't get very far.

Shane stepped in front of her, blocking the way. His face wore a hard look of determination, and she knew the reprieve had come to an end. Her resurrected fears joined forces with her full-blown panic. Her heart pounded in her chest and her blood ran cold. She couldn't quite catch her breath as she fought for some semblance of control over her rapidly escalating dread.

"We have to talk about—" The words stuck in his throat when he saw the terror that filled her eyes. He'd seen it there before, but now he knew why it was there. Now he knew the truth about Bobby.

She looked away, unable to maintain any type of eye contact with him. She injected as much finality into her words as possible. "We have nothing to discuss." Her eyes misted over. She fought to maintain control of her skyrocketing fears. "You made your true feelings perfectly clear when we were in graduate school. You may have finally explained your reasons for walking out, but that doesn't change anything. You were definite about not having anyplace in your life for me."

She blinked away the tears that brimmed in her eyes and started to trickle down her cheeks. "I took your words to heart and have since made a life for myself. So you see, we have nothing to discuss." She could not stand another moment of the churning sickness that threatened to overtake her resolve. She turned away from him and ran up the stairs to her room.

Her entire body shook violently as she sat on the edge of the bed. She made a futile attempt to untie the knots twisting in her stomach. She was sinking deeper and deeper into a hole she'd never be able to dig her way out of. She loved Shane, but that didn't change anything. A sob caught in her throat. Nothing mattered to her as much as her son. She'd do anything to protect him.

She heard the door open, then Shane's footsteps as he crossed the room. A cold terror cut through her. The walls closed in around her. This was it. She tried to gulp in enough air to settle the fear making its way up her spine. She opened her eyes and focused on his face. One look was all it took. Any hope that he didn't know the truth vanished.

"We have things to talk about—and the number-one item on the list is Bobby and his future." He broke eye contact with her. The fear that showed through her tears grabbed his heart. He clenched his jaw in renewed determination. There could be no turning back.

"About Bobby... He's my son, isn't he?"

She squeezed her eyes shut as the almost unbearable pain ripped through her body. He sounded so unemotional, so distant.

"Answer me, Cynthia. He's my son, isn't he?"

She managed a barely audible whisper. "Yes."

He knew what the answer would be, but it didn't prevent the hard lump that caught in his throat when he heard her say it. He couldn't stop the words that spilled out of him, half confusion and half anger. "Why, Cynthia? Why didn't you tell me you were pregnant? Why didn't you let me know I had a son?" And the most damaging of all. "Even after we made love last night, you still kept it from me." He shook his head, unable to comprehend how she could have done such a horrible thing. "Why?"

Years of pain and failed attempts to dismiss Shane from her life came out in an emotional rush. "He's my son. My life. You told me there was no room in your life for me. Since you don't have room for me, you couldn't possibly have any room for a child. I won't let you reject him the way you did me. I won't allow you to hurt Bobby the way you hurt me.''

Tears streamed down her cheeks. ''He's just a little boy, Shane. He's an innocent little boy who has no involvement in our past.'' Sobs wrenched her body now, as she blurted out her worst fear. ''Please don't tear his world apart by trying to take him from me.''

Shane recoiled as if he'd been struck. Total bewilderment filled his words. ''Take him away from you?''

''Please don't bring a custody suit.'' The very real fears that had been living inside her from the moment she realized she was in his house finally pushed her to the edge of hysteria. Her features contorted in anguish. She hurled her words at him. ''If you do anything to hurt him, I swear I'll never forgive you as long as I live.''

The depth of her emotional outburst shocked him, but not nearly as much as the meaning of her words and the pain surrounding them. Shane knew he had hurt her, but had no idea how much until now. His intention to straighten out his own life and identity before he could subject anyone else to the ambiguity of his world had cost him dearly. He had paid with the first five years of his son's life—Bobby's first step, his first word, watching him grow to a toddler and then to this bright little boy filled with curiosity and adventure. It had also cost him the only woman he had ever loved. Was it too late to repair the damage? He didn't know.

He studied the anxiety-filled face before him, the face of a woman who had threatened and pleaded with him all in one breath. And she now seemed to be holding that breath, waiting for him to say or do something. He didn't know what to say. He saw her emotional need, but the anger and resentment still churned inside him. He expelled a long breath, releasing some of his anger at the same time.

"Maybe this would be better discussed in the morning after a good night's sleep."

She pulled herself together and shoved aside her trepidation. She wasn't sure where the pocket of courage had come from, but she gratefully seized it. She had to tell him the rest, not leave any loose ends. "I plan to look for a house for Bobby and me first thing in the morning. I need to get Bobby settled in day care for the summer, then I'll be enrolling him in first grade in the fall. As soon as I find us a house, I'll be looking for a job."

She paused to gather her thoughts, wanting to make sure she clearly expressed herself so there could be no doubt about what she meant. "Regardless of what type of understanding you and I reach, it will not alter my need to get Bobby settled into a stable and permanent environment as quickly as possible."

He stared at her a moment longer, giving away nothing that was going through his mind. "We'll talk in the morning." He left the room, closing the door behind him.

The initial confrontation was over. The most difficult part had been handled. Shane knew that he had a son and that she and Bobby would be moving out of his house as soon as possible. Unfortunately Cynthia's sense of relief did not extend to the ache in her heart. The important thing now was to establish what kind of relationship Shane wanted with his son—and how to tell Bobby that Shane was his father.

The problem was far from resolved, but at least everything was finally in the open. There were no more secrets, no more fears of what might come out—only the fear of what would happen now. She rose from the edge of the bed. Her heavy sigh of despair told her nothing good could possibly come out of what had happened. She choked back a sob as she turned toward the bathroom, her sorrow almost more than she could bear. She hadn't taken more than two steps when the bedroom door flew open and Shane burst in. A sick lump lodged in her throat.

The determination on his face said it was the take-charge Shane Fortune who'd just entered the room. The same tenacity filled his voice. "This won't wait until morning. We have serious matters to work out, and we need to do it now. Bobby is my son, and I won't be left out of any more decisions concerning his future. We'll start with day care and his school."

It was the worst possible move he could have made. She matched his aggressive attitude with one of her own. Juggling single parenthood with a demanding full-time career had forced her to become her own person very quickly. The last thing she needed was Shane Fortune making her decisions for her, especially where her son was concerned. There was no longer any need for caution in order to preserve secrecy. She came out fighting like a mother bear protecting her cub.

She cut off anything further he might have intended to say and made no attempt to hide her displeasure. "I've managed just fine from the day you kicked me out of your life. Bobby is a happy child. He's well cared for and knows he's loved. I can handle all our needs without any help from you." She glared at him, aggressively leaning forward to show him that she refused to be intimidated.

If he thought he could easily get custody of Bobby, she would show him just how big a fight he'd have on his hands. She felt as if she was fighting for her own life, as well as her son's. "I'm willing to work with you to set up a convenient visitation schedule, but I will *not* be dictated to about how my son is to be raised!"

His level of anger, along with his volume, rose to match hers. "Do I need to remind you that Bobby is my son, too? Something that you *neglected* to mention to me until I forced it out of you?''

''I will not have my son's life upset any more than it already has been simply because you have decreed that it should be so. You may have the Fortune name, influence and money, but I will not allow you to run over me as if I were nothing more than a nuisance in the way of your plans.''

They glared at each other, the air between them charged with anger and passion.

''What's wrong, Mommy? Why are you and Shane mad?''

''Bobby…'' The sound of her son's voice sent an adrenaline surge through Cynthia, followed closely by a raw edge of panic. She had been so absorbed in her confrontation with Shane that she hadn't heard Bobby enter the room. How much had he heard? ''Uh, I'm sorry, honey. We didn't mean to wake you. We…'' She glanced uneasily at Shane, then back at her son. She knelt next to him, brushed his tousled hair away from his face and gave him a reassuring smile. ''We were discussing some business and I guess we got a little loud.''

She took Bobby's hand and started for the door. ''Come on. I'll tuck you in bed again.''

Shane watched as Cynthia led Bobby back to his bedroom. He'd been totally unnerved by their heated confrontation. He had never seen that side of Cynthia before, a woman who dug in and fought for what she wanted. It was a trait he knew well, for it was the same way he tackled things. He also saw the unconditional love Cynthia had for her son, and the trust in Bobby's eyes when he believed what his mother had told him.

The situation was precarious at best. Her emotion-laden words of earlier flooded through his mind. *He's just a little boy, Shane. An innocent little boy who has no involvement in our past. Please don't tear his world apart.* She was right. He couldn't allow Bobby to be the center of controversy between himself and Cynthia—a controversy that should never have existed. They should have been working as a team, rather than at odds with each other.

He loved her and wanted them to be a real family— Cynthia, himself and their son. It was the missing piece to his life, one he'd thought would not fit, but now realized had fit perfectly all along. He frowned as dark clouds began to gather overhead again. Cynthia had already made it clear that she was not in any mood to discuss a compromise. Perhaps it would be better left until morning, after all, when cooler heads prevailed.

When Cynthia returned to her room, it was obvious that she was still upset about their argument waking Bobby and in no mood to continue with it. He tried to ease the tension by projecting an upbeat manner.

"You've done a great job of raising Bobby. He's terrific."

Caution surrounded her words as she replied, "Thank you."

"Well—" he glanced nervously at the door "—perhaps a good night's sleep is what we both need." He started to leave the room, then paused and turned back toward her. "I'm looking forward to dinner tomorrow night with Riley, Isabelle, you and Bobby." He looked hopefully at her then turned toward the door again. "Good night, Cynthia."

She didn't respond. She just stood silently and watched as he left her room. She didn't know what to think. Did he intend to take Bobby away from her with a legal battle? The man she'd fallen in love with all those years ago wouldn't do that. The man she'd accompanied to the reservation certainly wouldn't do that. And the man she'd made love with last night wouldn't do that. But the man who'd just left her bedroom? She didn't know what to expect from him. She wasn't even sure who he was.

"Now, be very quiet. We don't want to wake Shane. He needs his rest," Cynthia whispered as she took Bobby's hand and started down the stairs. They left quickly through the front door and went to her car. She'd been a nervous wreck from the moment she'd opened her eyes that morning. She had to get out of the house before Shane could corner her. There was no way she could handle a repeat of the previous night's heated confrontation.

Bobby looked up at her, clearly confused. "Where are we going?"

"First we're going to have breakfast." She buckled his seat belt, making sure it was secure before she slid behind the steering wheel. "Then we're going to spend the entire day together. We're going to look at houses this morning. We'll find one with a nice swimming pool. Then we'll have lunch—maybe a picnic in the park. And this afternoon we can go to a movie. How does that sound?"

She drove down the street. Some of her tension drained away when they turned the corner and were out of sight of Shane's house. She was glad they'd been able to leave without encountering him. She glanced at Bobby and tried to shove away her guilty feelings about taking him house-hunting with her, something she knew wasn't what a little boy considered a fun thing. She would make it up to him with the movie.

The day went by smoothly—except for the anxiety over what would happen when they returned to Shane's house that evening. They looked at several rental houses, two of which she really liked. They had their picnic in the park and went to a movie. After the movie they looked at two more houses. Then they had dinner. It was going on six o'clock when they returned to Shane's house.

As soon as they stepped through the front door, Shane jumped up from the chair where he'd obviously been waiting. The expression on his face told her he was both impatient and angry. She stiffened her resolve. It would do him no good.

His words demanded more than asked. "Where have you been all day? You went sneaking out of here this morning without a word about your plans."

Her voice was soft as she spoke to Bobby. "Why don't you go upstairs and put on your swimsuit? We'll go into the pool in a little bit. Okay?"

His face lit up at the prospect. "Okay." He ran up the stairs.

She watched until he was out of sight, then turned a hard glare on Shane. "I hardly think walking out the front door is *sneaking*. Besides, I wasn't aware that I needed to clear my plans with you." She presented a cool composed exterior that totally belied the nervous tremors charging in all directions inside her. "Bobby and I went house-hunting this morning, then decided to make a day of it by going to a movie this afternoon."

"House-hunting?" His expression almost made it seem as if he didn't understand the meaning of her words.

"I fail to understand your surprise, especially since I informed you of my intentions last night."

Shane sidestepped her well-aimed comments. "Riley canceled for dinner tonight. He's not feeling well. We're supposed to meet Isabelle at the restaurant in less than half an hour."

"Then you'd better hurry."

"Me?" The surprise spread across his face. "What

about you? You and Bobby are supposed to have dinner with us.''

''Bobby and I have already had our dinner.'' It was a definitive statement and did not reveal any hint of her inner thoughts or feelings. She had to glance away when she saw the very real disappointment that filled his eyes.

''I see.'' His words were as devoid of emotion as hers.

''Mommy?'' Bobby called from the top of the staircase. His voice contained a sense of urgency. He hurried downstairs, his gaze darting between Cynthia and Shane. ''Are you and Shane going to fight again?''

His words cut through the thick cloud of troubled emotions. She saw the distress covering his little face and it tore at her heart. She knelt down and enveloped him in a loving hug. Her words were soft and comforting. ''No, honey, we aren't going to fight again.'' She glanced up at Shane and saw the embarrassment on his face that told her he, too, had no interest in pursuing the conversation in front of Bobby.

''I, uh...I have to get going.'' Shane took his car keys from his pocket, turned and left through the kitchen.

Fifteen minutes later he arrived at The Camel Corral to find Isabelle waiting for him. He greeted his sister with a smile and a kiss on the cheek, making sure he projected a manner that said nothing was amiss. ''Have you been waiting long?''

''No, I just got here.'' She looked around, her forehead creased in confusion. ''Riley told me he couldn't make it, but I thought Cynthia and Bobby would be with you.''

Shane immediately retreated behind his facade of calm control. ''No. I guess we got our signals crossed. They have other plans.''

Isabelle and Shane were shown to their table at the popular steak house by the hostess. "Angelica will be your server this evening. Enjoy your meal."

As soon as the hostess was out of earshot, Isabelle leaned across the table toward Shane. Her voice was barely above a whisper. "I suppose you've heard the rumor about Angelica Dodd and Riley. When Brad told me—" She stopped midsentence when she saw Angelica approaching their table.

Shane was glad for the interruption. He'd already heard the story from Cynthia. He really didn't want to participate in what was clearly gossip. He was worried about Riley. He'd tried to get through to his brother, to make him accept the seriousness of the situation, but his words had fallen on deaf ears.

Shane and Isabelle enjoyed a leisurely dinner and were finishing their coffee when Link Templeton approached the table.

Link nodded curtly at Shane. He cast an almost shy glance at Isabelle before focusing on Shane. "I thought you'd want to hear this from me personally, rather than secondhand. We've just arrested Riley for Mike Dodd's murder."

"You what?" Shane jumped to his feet, anger surging through his veins.

"I'm sorry, but my hands are tied. The evidence is just too damning to ignore any longer." Link turned toward Isabelle. "I'm sorry it had to go down this way. The DA's office issued the warrant, and I had to follow through."

Angelica had been standing behind Link. She grabbed his arm. "You...you've arrested Riley?" Her features registered stunned disbelief. Then she crumpled to the floor.

Shane immediately hunkered down beside her. He checked her pulse and her breathing. A minute later she came to. Her bewildered gaze darted from face to face. She tried to sit up. "What...what happened?"

Shane put his hand against Angelica's shoulder, holding her in place. "You fainted. I want you to stay right where you are. I'm going to call for an ambulance."

She shook off his restraint and sat up. "No, I'm all right."

"Don't argue with me, Angelica. I'm a doctor, which makes me in charge of this. I want you to go to the hospital and get checked out."

Angelica's voice bordered on the edge of panic. "I'm fine, honest. It's Riley—you've got to do something!" She grabbed the front of Shane's jacket, her eyes pleading with him. "You've got to get him out of jail."

As soon as Shane had satisfied himself that Angelica was okay, he turned his commanding presence to Isabelle and barked out orders. "You're coming with me. You watch Bobby. Cynthia and I are going to the sheriff's station."

He drove straight home, pulled up in the driveway, charged in the front door and yelled, "Cynthia!"

The urgency in Shane's voice carried throughout the quiet house, startling Cynthia. She set her book on the nightstand and hurried out into the hallway to the top of the staircase. She looked down and immediately spotted the distress on Shane's face and Isabelle's. A jab of apprehension darted through her body. She rushed down the stairs. "What's wrong?"

"Isabelle's going to watch Bobby. You're coming with me." He grabbed her hand and started for the front door.

"Wait a minute!" Cynthia tried to free her hand from his grasp. Something was terribly wrong. She'd never seen Shane so upset and unglued. "What's going on?"

"I'll explain en route." He dashed out the door with Cynthia running to keep up with his long-legged stride.

A minute later they were in his car and headed down the street. Shane's words were clipped. "They've arrested Riley for Mike Dodd's murder. You're an attorney. You've got to do something. You've got to get him out of jail."

She sat in stunned silence for a moment, then asked, "When did this happen?"

"Just a little while ago. Link Templeton located us at the restaurant right after Riley had been taken in."

"Shane…" She tried to choose her words carefully. She could see how distraught he was and she didn't want to add to it. "I'm a corporate attorney. I did a little bit of criminal litigation in Illinois, but I'm not a criminal lawyer, and that's what you need."

"There's got to be something you can do. You said you passed the Arizona bar exam, so you're licensed to practice law in this state." He turned his anguished gaze on her for a moment. "There has to be something you can do, Cynthia. Something."

She heard the panic in his voice and saw the plea in his eyes. This was a completely different Shane Fortune. He was totally distressed and seemed to be emotionally scattered. A sharp contrast to the normally dynamic, controlled and self-contained man she'd always known. This Shane Fortune was reaching out. He seemed to genuinely need her help. She'd never known him to ever truly *need* anyone before.

She projected a confident manner and a comforting smile, hoping to ease his obvious anguish. "I'll do everything I can."

He pulled into the parking lot at the sheriff's station,

and they rushed inside. Shane started making demands. Cynthia put a calming hand on his arm to stop him.

"You brought me here to do something, so let me do it. Riley is entitled to have an attorney present before they question him. I want you to sit down, take a deep breath and let me handle this." She turned him in the direction of some chairs and gave a gentle shove.

When she was satisfied that he was going to stay seated, she switched her attention to the desk sergeant. Her voice and manner told of her professionalism. She spoke with conviction, without being antagonistic. "My name is Cynthia McCree. I'm the attorney representing Riley Fortune. I want to see my client immediately."

Ten

___

Shane nervously paced the living-room floor, pausing every few minutes to check the time. It had been a miserable night of tossing and turning without much sleep, only this time Riley had been the cause, not Cynthia. And now the morning seemed to be going by at a snail's pace.

By the time he and Cynthia had arrived home from the sheriff's station, it had been well after midnight. The arraignment had been set for ten that morning. He'd allowed Cynthia to convince him to stay home and let her handle it—and that now seemed to him to have been a very bad idea. He checked his watch again. His raw nerves touched off his barely contained apprehension. He clenched his jaw and took a deep breath in an attempt to bring some sort of control to his raging anxiety. It was nearly noon and there hadn't even been as much as a phone call.

Just then he heard the sound of a car. He yanked open the front door and hurried out to the porch. His spirits sank. Cynthia was alone.

"Where's Riley? What happened?"

"Calm down, Shane." He looked as if he'd been running on pure adrenaline. "Riley's been released on bail."

Shane followed her into the house. The urgency still clung to his words. "Then where is he? Is he still at the sheriff's station?"

"I tried to bring him back here, but he insisted that I take him home. He said he wanted to be alone and that he'd give you a call later." She saw some of the distress leave his face.

"That's a relief. Is he okay?"

She set her attaché case on the table. "Other than being tired and understandably depressed, he's fine." She took off the jacket of her business suit and draped it across the back of a chair, then turned around. She studied him for a moment before speaking.

"Listen to me, Shane. You need to hire a top-notch criminal attorney to handle Riley's case. I was able to get him out on bail, but I'm not qualified to mount a defense in a first-degree-murder trial. I'll help you find someone if you'd like, but you need to do it quickly. This case is scheduled to go to trial in sixty days, and that's not much time."

Shane expelled a sigh of relief. "Thanks for everything you've done. I really appreciate it. I never dreamed they would actually arrest Riley. The whole thing is absurd." He took her hand and gave it a squeeze. "But thanks to you he's out of jail. I'm sure everything's going to be fine now."

He may have been putting up a good front, but she saw right through it. He was being pulled in too many directions. His medical practice, the Children's Hospital construction, his volunteer work with the Native American community and his rounds on the reservation took a lot of his time. He'd also single-handedly taken on the battle to regain control of Lightfoot Plateau. And now there was Riley's arrest and upcoming trial to add to the list. It was too much to expect of anyone. She refused to allow her thoughts to wander to the added stress of their as-yet-unfinished confrontation about his being Bobby's father.

"I was at a real loss about what to do and there you were." He pulled her into his arms and held her. She felt his need. She put her arms around his waist and responded to the honest emotion. It was a shared moment of tender caring, quite unlike the incendiary desire that usually resulted from his touch.

She knew that no matter how strong a man was, there came a time when he needed someone he could depend on, someone he could lean on for emotional support. It was the first time he'd allowed her to see his vulnerability, to touch the man inside. In spite of all their difficulties, it made the love she'd been refusing to acknowledge grow even more.

And it also frightened her.

She broke off what was quickly moving away from the moment of tender caring and toward a sensually comfortable interlude. "I need to change my clothes, then fix Bobby some lunch. I'm sure he's starved by now." She grabbed her attaché case and jacket, then hurried up the stairs.

She closed the door to her room and sat on the edge of the bed. The emotionally charged atmosphere surrounding Riley's arrest had momentarily taken the focus off her duel with Shane over Bobby. Now that Riley was out of jail, she feared the battle would be resurrected full force. A cold shiver told her she had no stomach for a fight, but she could not let down her guard. She quickly changed into a pair of shorts and a pullover shirt.

She went straight to the kitchen to start lunch. Bobby followed her. "I'm hungry. Shane said he was going to fix lunch, but he just kept looking out the window. He kept asking where you were. Were you lost, Mommy?"

"No, I wasn't lost. I was doing some business with Shane's brother, and it took longer than we thought. Shane was worried about his brother and anxious to find out what happened." She knelt down next to Bobby. "I'm sure he meant to fix you lunch."

Shane entered the kitchen carrying his car keys. "I've got to go to the hospital. I had meetings this morning that were rescheduled for this afternoon. I can't put them off any longer."

"What should I tell Riley if he calls? Should I have him call you at the hospital?"

"I'm wearing my pager, but I'll be pretty much un-reachable unless it's an emergency. Would you tell him I should be home by eight o'clock and will call him then?"

"Sure."

She watched as Shane disappeared through the door into the garage. Her tensed muscles relaxed a little. He would be gone all afternoon and part of the evening. They wouldn't be engaging in another battle of wills over Bobby—at least not today. They both needed a break from the stress and tension.

She fixed Bobby lunch, then they spent a quiet hour together reading a new book she'd bought for him. She listened to him carefully sound out new words as he read each sentence. He was such a bright and well-adjusted lit-tle boy. And now he was in danger of having his entire world turned upside down.

A wave of sorrow washed through her. Bobby's ques-tion about her argument with Shane had continued to cir-culate through her mind. He obviously knew something was wrong. How could she keep him from being hurt? She had to do something. Perhaps if she could manage to set the emotional aspect of things aside—approach Shane with logic—they would be able to come to some sort of amicable agreement about Bobby. A tremor made its way up her spine. Her innocent son had to be protected at all cost, but she didn't know how to do it now that Shane knew the truth.

Bobby read the last sentence in the book, then looked up at her questioningly. She gave him a warm smile. "That was very good. Your reading gets better every day."

"Can I go swimming now, Mommy?"

"You sure can."

They spent the rest of the afternoon in the pool, part of the time in play and part in instruction. And all the while Cynthia continued to run everything through her mind as she desperately searched for a workable plan to present to Shane when he got home. She fought to keep her soaring anxieties under control. She could not let Bobby sense her distress. Whatever she and Shane came up with, it would have to be presented to Bobby in an atmosphere of agreement and cordiality. There could be no hint of animosity.

A wave of sorrow washed over her. She loved Shane very much, yet she found herself in the horrible position of having to treat him like a hostile witness at a trial. If only her love could be reciprocated. They could be a family—a real family just as they should have been all along. She shook away the inappropriate thoughts. Wishing would not make it so. She had to deal with reality.

In spite of the brief interruption caused by Riley's arrest, it was something that could not be put off until a more convenient time. There was no such thing as a *convenient* time to introduce her son to his father and determine what the future held for all of them. A sick feeling lodged in her stomach. She sent up a silent prayer that Shane would continue to keep their personal conflict to themselves.

She kept a close eye on Bobby during the afternoon and evening, but he gave no indication that anything was bothering him. He didn't make any further comments about the argument that had woken him or his concern about Shane and her being mad at each other. She tried to convince herself that Bobby had forgotten the incident, but it was a waste of time. Bobby was a very bright, perceptive child. She wanted to believe he had forgotten, but in her heart she knew it wasn't so.

It had been an emotionally exhausting day for her, starting with Riley's arraignment and carrying through an afternoon and evening of building trepidation. It had taken an additional toll on her nerves to present an upbeat carefree front to Bobby. She was finally able to relax a little after she had him tucked safely in bed.

It would serve no purpose for Shane and her to continue arguing about Bobby's care and upbringing. There had to be some middle ground they could reach, some way to resolve things in a rational adult manner. She tried to pack her runaway emotions into some form of logic. She dealt with legal matters in a dispassionate way as part of her job. Surely she could apply that same ability to her personal life.

Shane had come under a lot of stress with Riley's arrest, and she didn't want to add to that pressure. A nervous jitter made its way through her body, then settled in her stomach. She couldn't spend every waking hour in terror of what might happen. It wasn't good for her and it certainly wasn't good for Bobby to have the air filled with that type of tension. The uncertainty surrounding Bobby's future had to be stopped. She sat quietly in the den, trying to formulate exactly what she would say when Shane returned home.

It seemed only minutes later when she heard him enter the kitchen from the garage. She looked at her watch, surprised to find that she'd been sitting there for an hour. A cold shiver darted up her spine. She felt his gaze and knew he was watching her. A tremor preceded the sick churning in her stomach. She took a calming breath, then looked up.

He stood in the doorway, staring at her. His drawn face showed stress lines. He looked as if all the resolve had been knocked out of him and he didn't know where to turn. In a heated instant her own fears disappeared and her heart went out to him. She wasn't sure what to say. "You look tired."

He sank onto the couch next to her and emitted a weary sigh. "My meeting just kept dragging on and on. I finally told them we'd have to finish at a later date."

"I didn't hear from Riley."

"He paged me at about five o'clock. We talked for half an hour. He said to tell you he really appreciates your getting him out on bail."

She gave a soft chuckle and at the same time expelled some of the tension building inside her. She was relieved that Shane didn't seem to be any more anxious than she was to renew their argument. "I know. He must have told me at least a dozen times on the way to his house."

"I think the seriousness of all this is finally beginning to sink in for Riley." Shane turned toward her and cupped her chin in his hand.

His touch sent a warm tingle of pleasure through her body, causing her a sharp intake of breath. It took all her reserve strength to keep from putting her arms around him. She looked into his eyes and saw his conflicting emotions, but couldn't find anything negative. Her heart beat a little faster and her pulse quickened.

Shane's voice dropped to a soft intimacy. "I want to thank you, too. I guess I wasn't thinking very clearly last night when we arrived at the sheriff's. I would have ended up making a mess of things. I don't know what I would have done without your help." He stroked her cheek with this fingertips. "Without you."

She tried to quell the little ripples of delight that danced across her skin in response to his touch. His words sent a ray of optimism through her. "I'm glad I was able to help." Did she dare believe that this was a sign they could work out their conflicting positions concerning Bobby in an amicable manner?

He glanced around the room. "Where's Bobby? Has he already gone to bed?"

"Yes, he's been asleep for almost an hour." Her hopes crashed. She braced herself for the inevitable. She had thought for a minute that they could postpone the discussion until morning or at the very least ease into the discussion. But apparently not.

A slight frown wrinkled his forehead. "I wanted to be home before he went to bed."

"Why?" She admonished herself for snapping out the question too quickly. This was not a time for hostility.

He stared at her. "Because I wanted to say good-night to my son, that's why."

A hard lump formed in her throat. She tried to swallow it, but was not very successful. She fought to keep the anguish out of her voice, also without much success. Her anxiety gave rise to renewed panic. "He doesn't know yet, Shane. I realize I should have told him this afternoon, but every time I tried to put the words together, they turned into a jumbled mess in my mind and I couldn't get them out of my mouth.''

A hard shiver raced through her body. ''Give me time to figure out how to tell him.'' She pleaded with her tone of voice as much as with her words. ''Please don't shatter his world.''.

Shane slipped his arm around her shoulders and pulled her close to his side. His manner was noncombative, his words sincere. ''Between Riley's predicament and our confrontation about Bobby, I've had a lot to think about today. Riley's situation is under control for the moment, so it's time to handle *our* problem. Bobby's a great kid. You've done a terrific job of raising him. He's a boy any father would be proud of—and that certainly includes me.''

A huge wave of relief washed over her. He'd made a straightforward statement without any recriminations. Was it possible that the crisis had passed? ''Thank you. I'm very proud of him.'' The words had come out in a whisper. It was the second time he'd told her his feelings about Bobby.

Her moment of reverie was short-lived, as her doubts and concerns leapt to the surface again. Had she read too much into what he'd said? Was she allowing her hopes and fears to color her judgment? She was scared to death that she would make a mistake, would somehow misinterpret his words and make the situation worse than it already was—if that was even possible. The fully revived tension was almost more than she could handle.

Shane turned toward her. He heard the renewed wariness in her voice and saw it in her eyes. He had spent a good deal of the afternoon and evening trying to corral his thoughts and emotions as they vacillated between Riley's arrest and discovering a son he'd never known.

Anger had surged through him when Cynthia had confirmed his suspicions about Bobby, but the time he'd just spent away from her had given him time to go over the facts in his mind. He vividly recalled the alarm in her voice and the nearly paralyzing fear in her eyes when she pleaded with him not to try to take Bobby away from her. It tore at his heart to see her so distraught. Realizing the depth of that distress and her genuine dread that he might actually try to do such a thing had landed a solid emotional blow to his senses and helped to clear his head.

He had no one but himself to blame. No matter how angry he was, it always came back to him. In the cold light of reality he could certainly understand why she'd kept his son a secret and why she was so frightened of what he might do. That dark moment when he had chosen to cut her out of his life had grown to such unwieldy proportions that it had reached out and ensnared an innocent little five-year-old boy who didn't deserve to have this type of controversy in his life.

He nervously cleared his throat. "I've had some time to think about things today—about Bobby and about you." Her muscles tensed as she started to pull away from him. He held her tighter, refusing to release his hold on her. "I don't want to fight with you. Please let me finish." He cradled her head against his shoulder.

"I'm so sorry for what I've put you through. I had no idea how deeply I had hurt you or the turmoil you've been carrying around with you the past six years." He felt her tense muscles begin to relax and became aware of her breathing. It was almost as if she had been holding her breath until that moment. He placed a tender kiss on her forehead. "We'll take things one step at a time. The first step is my asking you to forgive me for what I did."

The elation soared through her body, but the moment

was short-lived. Was that all there was? He asked her to forgive him, then everything went back to the way it had been ten minutes ago? That was no good. They still had not resolved Shane's participation in Bobby's future.

Her words were cloaked in caution and her response was tentative. "Okay...suppose I forgive you for walking out on me six years ago. What happens then?"

He framed her face with his hands. He brushed a loving kiss across her lips, then folded her into his embrace. "Even though I long ago reconciled my conflicts over my dual heritage, I still couldn't see how any woman would ever fit into the type of life I'd carved out for myself." He felt her body stiffen. "I was as wrong about that as I'd been about everything else where you and I were concerned."

He kissed her tenderly on the forehead. "I thought I didn't really need anyone, but now I know differently. My life isn't complete without someone to share the sorrows, as well as the triumphs. I need you, Cynthia. And now there's Bobby—our son. The two of you make my life complete in a way I never thought possible and fulfill me more than anything ever has."

He pulled back far enough to be able to look at her. Her eyes glistened with tears, but the joy that emanated from her face was clear to see. Emotion swelled his heart to the point where he thought it might actually burst from his chest. "I love you, Cynthia. I love you so very much. I was too pigheaded to realize how much you meant to me until it was too late. I allowed you to go once before, but I won't make that mistake again."

She couldn't contain the tears of happiness that trickled down her cheeks. Her heart filled with the years of unspoken love. "You have no idea how I've longed to hear those words. I love you, too. I've always loved you."

He hugged her tightly. His heart soared on the wings of her love. "I want us to be a family, Cynthia, a real family—the three of us."

"Do you mean—"

"I mean—" a grin tugged at the corners of his mouth "—that you can stop looking at houses." The grin disappeared as he dropped a soft kiss on her lips. Everything about him turned very serious. "Marry me, Cynthia. Help me make this house a real home."

She could barely get the words out of her mouth. "Marry you?"

"I want us to get married as soon as possible. What do you say?"

"Yes...yes. Of course I'll marry you."

He hesitated a moment as a frown wrinkled his forehead. "About the wedding..."

"Is there a problem?"

"Did you want a big wedding? Maybe we should think about something small and intimate, just the immediate family."

"This is all so sudden. You haven't given me a chance to think about it at all. Do you have a preference?"

"With Isabelle's wedding coming up and all the preparations well under way, I wouldn't want to upstage that."

Cynthia nodded in agreement. "You're right. Besides, it's not like we're a couple of kids who are just starting out in life."

"What would you say to applying for our marriage license in the morning, then having an intimate little ceremony in two weeks for just the immediate family?"

She smiled at him. The love that swelled her heart matched the love in his eyes "I think that sounds perfect." A moment of uncertainty clouded her features. "I still need to tell Bobby that you're his father."

"I think we should tell Bobby together—first thing in the morning." He rose from the couch, then tugged on her hand until she was on her feet. He scooped her up in his arms and started walking toward the stairs. "But for now, what do you think about seeing if we can create a little brother or sister for him?"

She snuggled in his arms and closed her eyes. A contented smile played across her lips. "I think that's an excellent idea."

Shane carried her up the stairs and down the hall to his bedroom. Unlike all the other times they had made love, this time the passion and the heated desire were enhanced by their commitment of love and a lifetime together. He framed her face with his hands and gazed lovingly into her eyes.

"I never fully understood what was missing from my life. No matter how many things I took on, there was always a gaping hole that needed to be filled. Always the drive and the success, but never the fulfillment—until now." He brushed a tender kiss across her lips. "I love you, Cynthia. I love you so very much."

She closed her eyes and allowed the soft sensuality to wash over her. "I've always loved you. I think I—"

The emotion overwhelmed him to the point where he couldn't contain it. His mouth came down on hers, claiming it as his own as he allowed his love to flow between them. He caressed her shoulders, trailed his hands down her back, then pulled her hips tightly against his. Their tongues meshed together in a rush of desire.

Pieces of clothing fell quickly away as they tumbled onto the bed entwined in each other's arms. He pulled her on top of him, then slid his hand over her creamy smooth skin, from her shoulders as far down as he could reach. He recaptured her mouth. Everything about her excited him beyond his ability to comprehend it. A low groan somewhere between pleasure and need rumbled from his chest.

His touch left her nearly breathless, and his kiss took the rest away. She straddled his hips as he slowly entered the core of her femininity. A shudder passed through her body when his hard length reached the depths of her being. She gasped and fell forward, her body pressed against his as they remained joined as one. It was a union that had never had more meaning than it did now, a union born of love. He grasped her hips, urging her into a slow rhythm that quickly escalated as their passion took control.

Shane rolled her onto her back, carefully preserving the physical connection between them. The moist heat of her sex closed tightly around his rigidity. He thrust forward, his movements more urgent with each plunge. It would be difficult to tell whose breathing was more ragged as each gasped for air. Her legs wrapped around his hips, and she arched to meet each of his strokes with the same urgency.

Time had no meaning. Nothing existed for them at that moment other than the deep love they shared. It was as if the past six years of turmoil and loneliness had been erased with one magic wave of a wand, taking with it everything bad and leaving only the good. A moment later the building ecstasy exploded with a force more powerful than either of them had ever known.

Cynthia gasped as the convulsions started deep inside her and quickly spread through her body. She completely gave herself to the rhapsody that invaded every part of her consciousness. She barely had enough breath to utter in a husky whisper, "I love you, Shane...very much."

As if hearing those words was the only thing standing between him and the final moment of gratification, he held her tightly in his arms as he gave one last deep thrust. A shudder traveled through his body, followed by hard spasms of release. He fought to bring his breathing under control and find his voice.

"You are my life, Cynthia. I don't want to ever lose you again."

Cynthia handed the small bridal bouquet to Isabelle, who had accepted with pleasure when asked to be the maid of honor. She held out her hand, which Shane clasped lovingly in his. They turned to face the minister. The small chapel was filled with immediate family. Kate Fortune sat in the front row, making no attempt to hide an expression that said she knew more than she was saying about how and why Shane and Cynthia had gotten together again after six years.

Bobby stood next to Shane. His chest was puffed out and his face beamed with pleasure. He looked very grown-up wearing his first suit. It was an exact duplicate of Shane's charcoal gray pinstriped suit. He'd been so excited when Shane had asked him to be his best man. He held the wedding ring tightly in his hand.

The minister intoned, "Do you, Cynthia McCree, take this man…"

The squeeze from Shane's hand sent a loving flow of energy through Cynthia's body. She was still having a difficult time believing all this was true. Less than two weeks ago it seemed as if her entire world had collapsed around her. And now everything was perfect. She had never been happier. She returned Shane's squeeze, letting him know how much she loved him.

"Do you, Shane Lightfoot Fortune, take this woman…"

Shane still had difficulty believing everything that had happened. In a couple of minutes the culmination of all his desires would be realized—a wife he loved very much and a boy he was proud to call his son. They would be a family, a real family. He'd never been happier.

"By the power vested in me by the State of Arizona, I pronounce you man and wife."

Shane pulled Cynthia into his arms. "I love you, Mrs. Fortune. I love you very much."

"I love you, too. We'll have the rest of our lives together."

Bobby tugged on Shane's sleeve. "Where are we going on our honeymoon, Daddy?"

Cynthia and Shane looked at the eager little face staring up at them. "Well, son—" Shane tousled Bobby's hair and grinned at him "—I think we need to have a man-to-man discussion about this."

*   *   *   *   *

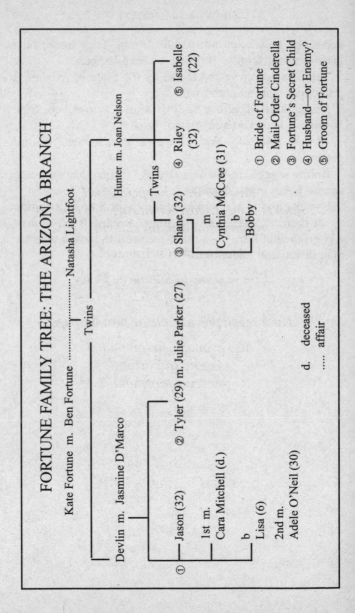

FORTUNE FAMILY TREE: THE ARIZONA BRANCH

Kate Fortune m. Ben Fortune

Devlin m. Jasmine D'Marco ········· Natasha Lightfoot ········· Hunter m. Joan Nelson

Twins — Twins

① Jason (32)

② Tyler (29) m. Julie Parker (27)

③ Shane (32)
m
Cynthia McCree (31)
b
Bobby

④ Riley (32)

⑤ Isabelle (22)

1st m.
Cara Mitchell (d.)
b
Lisa (6)
2nd m.
Adele O'Neil (30)

① Bride of Fortune
② Mail-Order Cinderella
③ Fortune's Secret Child
④ Husband —or Enemy?
⑤ Groom of Fortune

d. deceased
···· affair

*Find out what happens when
Riley Fortune discovers that Angelica Dodd is
pregnant with his child in*

Husband—Or Enemy ?

*Coming only to Silhouette Desire
in May 2002.*

For a sneak preview, please turn the page.

Also available next month is
Groom of Fortune
by Peggy Moreland

Husband—Or Enemy?

by

Caroline Cross

Riley Fortune narrowed his pale gray eyes against the shifting nighttime shadows as he focused his gaze on the service entrance of The Camel Corral some forty feet away.

Riley felt a surge of annoyance, which he did his best to shrug away. After all, what did he expect? That after three months of avoiding Angelica Dodd he could suddenly decide he wanted to see her and she'd instantly appear?

Well…yeah. The realization sent a faint smile—his first in more days than he could remember—curving across his brooding mouth. All right. So he was accustomed to women chasing after him, then dropping at his feet like so many overripe plums with hardly more than a snap of his fingers. So what?

So you know damn well Angelica's not like that. The only reason she succumbed to your charms, considerable

*though they may be, is that she was hurting—and because
you took advantage of her. Although even for you, seduc-
ing a woman only hours after her brother's death has to
be a new low.*

But then, nobody had ever mistaken him for a saint. A
fact that had been forcefully driven home a week ago when
he'd gone from being merely a suspect to actually being
charged with the same brother's murder.

But that was a subject for another day, he reminded
himself sharply, rolling his shoulders in an attempt to re-
lieve the knotted tension. Tonight's little drama involved
an entirely different kind of life-altering situation....

The restaurant door opened and another waitress exited.
And though this one was dressed exactly the way the others had been, Riley recognized her instantly.

Angelica? A sudden heaviness filled Riley's groin as a
vision of Angelica naked flashed through his mind. He
sucked in a breath. *Damn.* Why couldn't he quit thinking
about that night?

With an oath, he pushed himself away from his Cor-
vette, unable to stay still a second longer.

His abrupt movement drew his quarry's eye. She jerked
to a stop and a kaleidoscope of emotion—surprise, uncertainty, welcome, wariness—flashed across her vivid face.
"Riley?"

"Hello, Angelica."

She took a moment before she answered, slowly drawing an air of indifference around her like a cloak. "Well,
gosh. What are you doing here? That fancy car of yours
run out of gas?"

"We need to talk."

"We do, huh? About what?"

"We need to talk about Mike. I didn't kill him, Angelica."

She stared at him a moment, then gave a faint sigh and nodded. "For what it's worth, I believe you. So if that's all you want—" although her voice was offhand, her fingers shook as she tucked a wayward strand of hair behind her ear "—I'll be going. It's late."

The vulnerability revealed by that shaking hand rocked him. Almost as much as her matter-of-fact assertion of his innocence. He reached out without thinking and caught her by the arm. "Angel, wait."

A shudder went through her at his touch and she jerked away. "What do you want?" she demanded impatiently.

"I know you're pregnant. The baby's mine—we both know it."

"Oh, I know perfectly well that you're the father, Riley. What I can't believe is that you really think you can just show up and have some say in my life. You don't."

"The hell I don't. If there's one thing you can count on, it's that we Fortunes take care of our own."

"Just what is *that* supposed to mean?"

"Isn't it obvious? We'll have to get married. The sooner the better."

She stared at him in astonishment. "If that's your version of a proposal, the answer is no. And now, if you'll excuse me, I'm leaving. Before I say something we'll both regret." Not waiting to hear his reply, she walked resolutely toward her car.

Face set, Riley stood where he was. No matter what Angelica thought, this wasn't over, he thought grimly.

Not by a long shot.

In the past few weeks he'd lost an alarming portion of

his freedom, his faith in the justice system and what had been left of his reputation.

No matter what it took, he wasn't about to lose his son or daughter, too. And since Angelica was part of the package...

She'd just have to be persuaded to give him another chance.

* * * *

Don't forget Husband—Or Enemy?
and
Groom of Fortune
are on the shelves next month.

Welcome back to the Fortune dynasty

The drama and mystery of Fortune's
Children continues with a new
12-part book continuity series.

Fortune's Children: THE GROOMS
and
Fortune's Children: THE LOST HEIRS

The drama, glamour and mystery
begins with Fortune's Grooms,
five strong, sexy men surrounded
by intrigue, but destined for love
and marriage!

FC/RTLH